Spirit Hunter

Spirit Hunter

KATY MORAN

WALKER
BOOKS

First published in Great Britain 2010 by Walker Books Ltd
87 Vauxhall Walk, London SE11 5HJ

2 4 6 8 10 9 7 5 3 1

Text © 2010 by Katy Moran
Cover images: Girl © 2010 Clayton Bastiani/Trevillion Images;
Peonies © 2010 Gaby Wojciech/Photolibrary;
Tang Dynasty calligraphy © 2010 41–/Photolibrary

The right of Katy Moran to be identified as author of this
work has been asserted by her in accordance with the
Copyright, Designs and Patents Act 1988

This book has been typeset in Giovanni

Printed and bound in Great Britain by Clays Ltd, St Ives plc

British Library Cataloguing in Publication Data:
a catalogue record for this book is
available from the British Library

ISBN 978-1-4063-1728-2

www.walker.co.uk

www.katymoran.co.uk

This book is dedicated to (in order of appearance)

Zelie Birkbeck

Noah Macey

Nuala Johnstone

Barnaby Clark

Owen de Wilde

Evan Llewellyn

Lily Cooper

Flynn Hartford

Edie Hobson

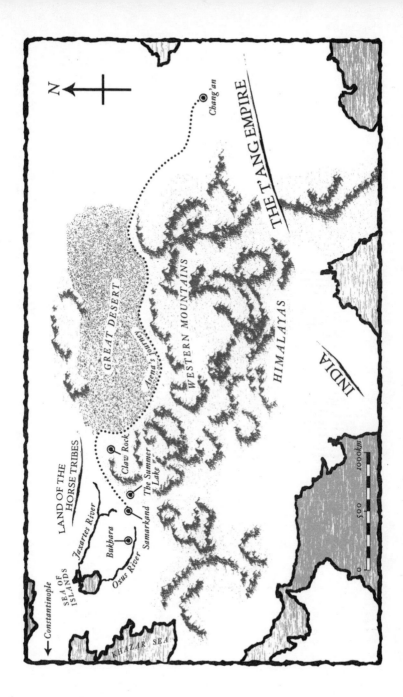

Prologue

*Chang'an, capital of the T'ang Empire,
around AD 665*

Swiftarrow knelt at the Empress's feet, bowing low. How long would she make him wait? His forehead pressed against the well-shone cedar floorboards, his right arm brushed the edge of a Persian carpet. To crush his irritation he counted, half listening to the jumble of voices and laughter. Artists, poets, well-known wits and historians claiming ancient knowledge: all flocked to the Empress whenever she wished to be amused.

"Such deep-black brush-strokes – ah, my dear! – and such exquisite misery" … "If you'd heard what she said next, Lady Xiang, you would have flushed scarlet…"

And all of them speaking more or less nothing but non-sense – terrified out of their senses, Swiftarrow thought. He tried to ignore the scent of hot rice wine mingling with steamed rose oil. Early-blooming peonies floated in porcelain bowls scattered about the Imperial chamber.

Below the clamour of chattering courtiers, Swiftarrow heard quick, nervy footsteps and panicked breathing. Servants, flitting about the chamber, removing flowers the moment they began to wilt, replacing them with fresh ones. The servants had every right to be afraid. Only the last ten-night a maid at the Xingqing Palace was drowned in a courtyard well. Why? A vase with a fingerprint that no one managed to wipe off before the Empress caught sight of it.

She treats men and women as nothing more than fleas – to be crushed with scarcely a thought. Swiftarrow squeezed his eyes shut, fighting anger. He had not killed so much as a fly since the summer of his fourth year, when his mother had died and he had been sent to the temple of the Forbidden Garden. *Seven, eight, nine, ten,* he counted.

"Rise, little Shaolin, my pretty pet." The Empress spoke in a girlish tone that sent a chill down the back of Swiftarrow's neck.

Very well, O Imperial Majesty. Let me hear your wisdom. He sat back on his heels, still kneeling, head bowed.

For the briefest moment, quiet settled on the chamber, and Swiftarrow felt the heat of many eyes watching him.

"What do you all stare at?" the Empress snapped. "Your mouths hang open like the maws of my golden carp when they wish to feed. It is desperately unappealing."

"Indeed Your Imperial Majesty is right," said a drawling, familiar voice. "I beg you, dear friends, do not look at the boy too long. He will grow conceited." Lord Fang:

how many years was it since Swiftarrow had last seen him? Seven? Or was it eight?

Eleven, twelve, thirteen, fourteen, he counted. *Don't let him anger you. Don't allow it.*

"Of course, Lord Fang. Surely the boy's conceit is not an accident of birth?"

Noise broke out again – mirthless terrified laughter, more chatter, but Swiftarrow did not bother sifting through the clamour to hear what reply Lord Fang made.

Most likely for the best, Swiftarrow thought, grimly. He pushed Lord Fang from his mind, hiding him away like an unwanted robe at the bottom of a clothes chest.

"Listen to me, boy," said the Empress. Her voice hissed like wind through a forest of bamboo. "I have a task for you." She paused, and Swiftarrow guessed she was smiling. He was not fool enough to look at her uninvited. "Word has reached me that far beyond the western desert my husband's barbarian subjects whisper of rebellion. From his sickbed, my esteemed husband has despatched one General Li to hunt down the Horse Tribes and destroy them." The Empress sighed. "Unfortunately, this Li has not the wit of a toad, and the Tribes, though they are filthy and foolish, are most excessively cunning. They are certain to evade him. I wish you to go with the general, O my little half-bred Shaolin, and make sure that he succeeds. It is essential to the happiness of my dear husband that you do so. Do you understand?"

The Horse Tribes, Swiftarrow thought. *She wants me to betray my own mother's people.*

But she was the Empress and what choice did he have? It was not only his life that hung in the balance, utterly at her mercy.

Swiftarrow paused for only the briefest moment.

"O Your Imperial Majesty, Light of Light, I shall do whatever you command or lose my life in trying."

The Empress laughed. "I know you will succeed. After all, I am sure you would not wish your beautiful sister to meet with any harm. Believe me, boy, life as a courtesan is full of danger. One has so many jealous rivals. Or at least I did but, as you can see, I have bettered them all. Let us hope the famed White Swan has the wit to do the same." She giggled. "Only pray she has not the ambition to take my place. If she does, I will be forced to have the teeth pulled out of her skull."

Swiftarrow drew in a long, steady breath, glad the Empress could not see his face but praying the sheer, cold depth of his rage did not show in his stance. *If you dare hurt my sister, O Imperial Majesty, I will make you sorry. I will find a way.*

"Autumn Moon has trained you well in the Forbidden Garden," the Empress went on, and then fell silent a moment, as if turning over a thought in her mind. "General Li is a prideful man: he must believe that I expect him to find the Tribes alone. So I should like you to do one other thing for me on your journey to the west, and Li will think it your only task."

"Your Majesty must only tell me, and it shall be done."

"The Shaolin have served me well of late. I wish to have

another one like you. When you ride to the west, boy, bring me a barbarian for Autumn Moon to teach. Half-bred or full-blooded, I care not. But I think it shall be of great use to me to have another Shaolin with the courage and horse-craft of the Tribes." The Empress laughed again. It sounded like broken glass. "Do you see, boy? I may be the wife of an emperor, but I still know my housekeeping. I have set a rat to catch a rat."

Part One

Along the Road

1

Asena
Summer pastures, a few days' ride from
Samarkand, two moons later

I lie with my face in the dust, head turned to one side. Stones and grit bite into my cheek, tickle my ear, but I cannot move. Arrows thump into the ground no more than a hand span away. The earth shakes with drumming hoofbeats. Men on horseback armed with spears and bows. A woman falls beside me, her face next to mine. Blood trickles from a corner of her mouth, thick and dark. Her eyes are open but she is dead: she has no spirit-horse and her body is nothing but an empty shell. Grey strands of hair hang across her brow, waiting for someone to brush them away. No one will.

How long have I got before they come for me? How long before I die?

Among the screaming and the din of battle, I hear soft, quick footfalls. I catch the rank scent of wet dog only stronger, sharper. Not dog.

Wolf.

Using the last of my strength, I turn my head. Here he is, dark and brindled grey with scarcely any white in his fur. A shadow-wolf. I should be afraid. I'm not. It is like looking down at my own hand. Light flickers about this beast as if he is made of fire, not flesh, bones and hunger like other wolves.

The wolf draws nearer, moving with quick, silent grace. He pays no heed to the dead woman at my side, even though the scent of her blood must still be hot and good. His eyes are bright, darker than a handful of earth after rain. I reach out with my mind, sifting through the wolf's inner self as I would with a mare or one of my uncle's hounds. He doesn't dream of the kill, or being safe and warm with his clan, or running free, like most of the wolf-kind, because he is not really a wolf: he is a spirit. My guide when I slip beyond a dream's edge and stray from the world of men; I am a shaman, and he is mine.

Keep watch, says my wolf-spirit, *or this time will come.*

When? I answer. *How can I stop it?*

But he is already gone.

I wake with a jerk, breathless. It's still dark in the tent. That dream again, stalking me night after night. I lie shivering, clutching the blanket about my shoulders. It's cold.

It's no ordinary dream. It is a message. Falling arrows and a dead woman? I don't like this. Who would?

"Help me keep danger from our fireside." My prayer is swept up with the thin trails of smoke still drifting from the

18

fireplace and out through the smoke-let in the top of the tent. Up to the sky, straight to the spirits.

I hope they listen.

Rolling over in the blanket, I sit up, peering across the shadowy tent at Mama, a sleeping hump wrapped in rugs, her spirit-horse a sleepy silver flicker just by her left shoulder. The place at her side is still empty. Baba and the rest of the men will be home with the next new moon, rich with spices and other treasures got for last year's fine foals, and tales from the Roads, too. Till then, Mama must sleep with no one to hold her. On the far side of the hearth, Shaman Tulan lies still beneath a mound of hides and rugs: he has been sleeping since we broke our fast yesterday morning.

He's just old, Mama said last night, trying to hide her swelling sorrow. We both know that Tulan is making ready to leave us for the next life. Where's his spirit-horse? Gone. He's not asleep, then. His spirit has left his body. My heart pounds. *Don't go*, I beg him silently. *You can't leave me yet. I'm not ready to do this alone, herding the souls of our people the way Shemi and I herd goats up the pasture.* I lean forwards, looking closer. The pile of rugs rises and falls gently, again and again: there is still breath in Tulan's body. He is not dead but only travelling again – away with his spirit-horse and his own eagle-guide in the World Above. I shiver, even wrapped in my blanket.

I push away my covers and lie listening to the rain, watching gnat-sized droplets fall through the smoke-hole above and sizzle in the hearth's embers. I hate waking before dawn. It's when the bad thoughts come creeping into my head like spiders, scuttling about till I've no hope of sleeping again.

Yesterday, when the sun rose above the eastern mountains, my friends rode out to hunt: Shemi, Tela, Yan and sour-faced Unnap.

"I think it's a shame you can't come with us any more," Tela said, not quite meeting my eye. "It's not fair you're forbidden to hunt." Her spirit-horse pranced, skittish, ears laid flat against her head. Tela tries to hide it, but she has been afraid of me since last summer, when old Tulan gave me the rites and I became a true shaman.

"No use mourning what can't be mended," I told her, forcing a smile.

"She would only scare away the beasts with her fiery souls," Yan called. He grinned at me but his smile was brittle like a crust of new ice on the Winter Lake. "You know the shaman can never hunt. Come, Tela, we cannot wait."

Yan helped Tela up into her saddle and they all rode away to the lake to shoot ducks. Like the rest of us, Tela has been riding since before she could walk. She is well able to mount by herself, but she just smiled at him.

Just as well my tribe forbids me to love a boy as Tela loves Yan, I tell myself. *At least I shall be spared such shameful weakness.* But tears burn my eyes and slip hot down my face. It is not fair. I did not choose to be born with the spirit of a wolf-cub leaping after me into the world. I did not choose to be born seeing the souls of men and women: silver spirit-horses bucking with joy or peaceful and still – always betraying to me folks' true thoughts and most secret feelings. My powers come at a cost: not only am I forbidden to hunt, I am also forbidden to love. When I was young, I asked Tulan why he did not have a woman and a tent of his own.

It is the way of our clan. It has always been so for the shaman. How could I look after the souls of our people if I were wildly in love with a girl? he told me, and smiled. *Or, old as I am now, how could I watch over our kin if I were kept busy being nagged and cosseted by a wife of many years?*

Fool of a girl! I tell myself. *Which of the boys would have you, anyway? They would be afraid of the spirits' anger. They would be afraid that the deer would all die before we could shoot them, or that the women would all fall barren and bear no more children. And even if that were not so, which of them should you choose?* I close my eyes and see the faces of all the boys in this tribe: my hare-brained cousin Shemi, and Yan who looks past me seeing only Tela. I can scarcely blame him because Tela is so fair and mild, with her thick shiny plaits and kind smile. Who else is there? Sly Unnap and his brother who is only five summers old.

No. I am shaman: I will never have a boy to love. It is my fate, and the truth of it sticks in my throat like a dry piece of meat.

2

Swiftarrow
A traders' inn, one day's ride from Samarkand

Sitting beneath a pistachio tree outside the inn, Swiftarrow opened his eyes, rubbing his aching legs. Darkness had fallen across the grimy courtyard, which was seething with men. Thousands upon thousands of them all crammed into this sprawling trader-inn. Smoke rose from the soldiers' campfires, veiling the stars. General Li's legion was a raggle-taggle mob: a muddle of untrained conscripts barely old enough to shave and battle-weary Horse Tribe half-breeds who rode with more grace than they could walk.

Half-breeds like me, yet I am not like them. Swiftarrow was only too aware that he sat in the saddle like a sack of rice – the Shaolin had taught him many skills, at home in the temple, but horse-riding was not one of them. *The Empress was wrong about that: I may have the blood of the Tribes, but I cannot ride.* Shame washed over him and he let out a long breath, pushing away the thought of it. On his own two feet he was lithe as a cat, so what did it matter? Swiftarrow sighed. How long had he been away, released from the world of men? He leaned back against the tree. A few hours at the very least.

He drew in a long breath, letting his eyes fall shut once more. He felt the heat of his *chi*, his life-force; it coursed through his veins, burning like fire. Good. He needed strength if he wished to speak with General Li. Swiftarrow could hear him from the far side of the courtyard, braying like an ass at the young T'ang recruits. At least the half-blood cavalry-men could pretend they did not understand enough to listen. Swiftarrow watched them hunching around their campfires, tossing bones over their shoulders, swigging mare's milk liquor.

Springing up, Swiftarrow stretched out his arms. He was ready. He knew how not to be seen. Breathing deeply, thinking of nothing, he picked his way through the straggle of soldiers and campfires, past the broken fountain. He paused by the largest group of men, listening. It always paid to listen.

"What did we do to deserve this trek across the desert, anyhow?" muttered one of the T'ang soldiers to the half-breed lounging at his side.

"It's a fool's errand," replied the half-breed. "Old Pork-belly may dream of hunting down the Tribes all he wishes, but they're cunning. They're quick. They know the ground here and we do not. He'll not find this nest of rebels unless he trips over it."

His T'ang companion laughed, and they began talking instead about one of the camp whores. Swiftarrow walked away, trying to ignore his wrath. His sister was a concubine, living to serve men like this – richer ones, but just as foul. *Keep to the Path of Peace*, he told himself: he could not raise his hand against a man in anger.

General Li lounged by the largest campfire, flanked by a pair of young T'ang conscripts. *Hiding their boredom to buy favour*, Swiftarrow thought. *Not so foolish as they look.*

"And so, of course, the Empress laughed," the general confided. "Lord Fang is very much a favourite of hers. One day, perhaps you boys shall meet him."

"We should be most honoured," said the oldest. Judging by the soldier's speech, it was clear he came from one of the great clan families. No doubt he had already met Lord Fang, Swiftarrow thought, most likely many more times than the general himself, but had wit enough to keep this quiet. Hidden in the shadows, Swiftarrow smiled. Everyone knew the general's father had been a merchant who made a pile of gold bigger than Mount Hua selling the feathers of exotic birds from the southern provinces. Li set great store by aristocratic blood. *What would he say if he knew of mine?* Swiftarrow wondered, smiling again, but bitterly.

The general laughed, passing the flask of wine. "Fear not, my boys. We'll hunt down those barbarians. They shan't be hard to find – we'll catch their stink from a day's ride off. We'll teach the Horse Tribes to defy the Empress, and you shall all return to Chang'an with much honour."

Fool, Swiftarrow thought. *The Tribes are scattered across the steppe like grass seeds on the wind. Does he think to find them all clustered together, waiting to be killed?* What was it General Li had done to arouse the Empress's displeasure, anyhow? Swiftarrow did not for a moment believe this fool's errand was the Emperor's idea: everyone knew the shaking sickness kept His Imperial Majesty in bed, one side of his face frozen and slack. So what had Li done? Spoken out of turn to an Imperial nephew? Outraged the modesty of a palace-favoured courtesan? That seemed unlikely: it was well known the Empress had no great fondness for her husband's courtesans, even though she herself had been his father's concubine. But General Li must certainly have transgressed in some way to earn such a heaven-forsaken mission across the desert. Ambushing the Horse Tribes? It was a hopeless task. Everyone knew the Tribes could outride a river in flood, and that they could melt away into nothing, hidden in forests and the wild mountains.

Swiftarrow stepped forwards, out of the shadows. Neither the general nor his audience managed to hide their shock. Swiftarrow dropped to his knees, bowing low to the ground.

"What do you want, half-breed?" said General Li.

Swiftarrow sat up, head still bowed in a show of respect. "O General, I must beg that you allow me to continue my search in Samarkand."

"Continue your search?" The general sneered, and his young soldiers laughed, obediently. "I wish you good fortune, boy. You have not yet met with great success, seeking out new flesh for your slithering Shaolin master."

For my Shaolin mistress, Swiftarrow thought, but it was not worth taking the trouble to correct him.

General Li drank deeply from his cup, swilled the wine about his mouth and spat the dregs onto the ground at Swiftarrow's knees. "I know not why Her Imperial Majesty prizes you Shaolin so high, sneaking around like rats. Chang'an seethes with holy men and women as it is. Why has the Empress sent you to find more?"

If only you knew I am really here to make sure you *find the Tribes.* Swiftarrow shrugged. "O General, you know I was given this task under the orders of our Divine Empress. We Shaolin are honoured to have her gracious admiration. I have been ordered to scour the furthest reaches of the empire for new blood, and I must do my duty."

"Your foolish quest is no concern of mine," snapped General Li. "Go as you will, boy, but return in seven days' time, or you shall be crossing the desert alone."

It would be my dearest pleasure to be rid of your company, Swiftarrow thought, but he said nothing, of course, and got to his feet, fading from their sight.

3

Asena
The World Above

I t's been a long, hot morning but now the milking is done. I leave the milk-pails by the hearth and stand still for a moment in the cool gloom of our tent. Shaman Tulan is gone, his blankets and rugs lying heaped on the ground. I smile as relief washes over me: *so my old friend is back in the world of men. For now, at least.* I can tell him about my dream after all. Will he be at the lakeshore again? He spends a lot of time by the water now. *It's the gateway to the World Below,* I think, and the relief drains away, replaced by cold dread. There will come a day when Tulan is not here, when he will never come back. There will come a day when I am the only shaman.

I must get away before Mama asks me to help her make the yogurt. If I'm asked to watch someone's squalling baby or fetch water, the day will shrink before me in a muddle of chatter and tea-drinking and skinning hares for the pot.

I will have to go without being seen – the skill I love dearest. Why – because it has nothing to do with my fate as shaman, or because it is so much fun? I don't know, but here I go, anyhow.

I run headlong through the camp, right past my cousin Shemi as he walks lazily to his mother's tent, trailing his feet, and he does not see me. I run past Otem and his small sister walking hand-in-hand to the lakeshore to fill buckets of water. Not one of them sees me. I am a shadow, a breath of wind. I am free. The chat and hum of camp fades as I reach the lakeshore trees. It is cooler here. I can go anywhere; I can do anything.

"Asena!"

I freeze. *Curses.* It is Mama, coming out of Aunt Zaka's tent. I sigh. Mama is the only one who can ever spot me once I've chosen not to be seen.

I go to her, shrugging. "What?"

Mama rests one long-fingered hand against the side of my face. Her touch is cool, but her spirit-horse is skittery, dancing around her shoulders like a freshly kindled flame, glowing with silver light. Much as she might try to hide it, Mama is always touched by fear when Baba goes away trading. "Where are you going in such a rush, my cub?" she says, speaking in Anglish. "What about the yogurt? Am I to make it alone again?"

Looking back at camp, I watch as Yan and Tela emerge from his mother's tent, hand-in-hand, each carrying an empty pail. They have been milking together. It is enough to make you spew. Sometimes it is so hard to swallow my jealousy. It's not that I want Yan – Tela is welcome to him. *I just wish—* Oh, it is useless to think of it.

"Well?" Mama says.

I reply in the tongue of the Tribes. I don't like speaking Anglish: I am set out as different already. I cannot love; I cannot hunt. I am shaman. I do not like being reminded of my foreign blood. "Tulan has woken. I must find him."

Mama sighs. I hate it when my mother looks at me like this, as if she sees another in my place. "Sometimes you put me in mind of my brother, with all this sneaking around, not being spotted by anyone save me," she says. "And I don't like it—"

"Your brother, the greatest thief in Constantinople?" I cut in. "Don't fear, Mama. I'm not sneaking to steal, only because I can't move without being given another task, and I must speak to Tulan—"

This time Mama cuts me off. "I know it," she says, glancing at Yan and Tela, who have stopped and set down their buckets near the great fire. Tela is standing on the tips of her toes, shiny black plaits hanging down her back, whispering into Yan's ear. Yan smiles. I glimpse a flash of sadness in Mama's eyes. "You carry more burdens than most girls your age. Asena, I know the rules are hard to bear, but never forget that being shaman is a gift as well. And one thing I have learned is that nothing good comes from dishonesty." She smiles. "Perhaps you should try asking for help every now and then. Shemi and little Aza can make the yogurt with me this morning. Now, go to Tulan in peace."

Mama is forever reminding me how much I love her.

Here he is, Shaman Tulan, sitting beneath a mulberry tree just a few paces from the lake's edge. He stares into the fire, wrinkled, dry old hands hanging loose in his lap. A pile of bones sits on the dusty earth before him, next to a bowl full of charred twigs and ash – I catch the smell of burnt juniper and the warmth of thyme.

Tulan does not move, even when I come closer and crouch right beside him: he is away again. His spirit-horse has gone wandering. *Did it drift up the mulberry tree to the World Above or sink down through glittering lake-waters to the World Below?*

I sit down at my teacher's side and wait. The bones are curved and yellowish: sheep shoulder blades. So Shaman Tulan wants to learn what is to come. By the time I see the flicker of his spirit-horse again, my legs ache with sitting still so long. But I have learned to be patient. The old man turns to smile at me, prodding the flames with a bent stick.

"So, Asena. I've been waiting." Tulan's eagle-guide appears, perching on his shoulder, eyes fierce, watching me. Tulan's gaze burns my skin. "You are troubled. What have you been dreaming of, Asena?"

"Death," I tell him, frowning. "Death and a battle. My wolf showed me." I shiver, even in the fire's heat. "It wasn't only men fighting with honour: there were women and brats, too. Was it a foretelling? Will it really happen?"

My old teacher tosses a mulberry twig into the fire. It crackles, catches light, glowing. He turns, meeting my eyes once more. "Not a foretelling but a warning," he replies. "Come, I've told you this before: wise men and women steer their own path – we are not just borne along wild and unsteady at the whim of the spirits, like a wall-dweller trying to ride a high-spirited stallion, as some folks would have you believe. But your dream was a warning from the spirits, all the same, and we should heed it. We must go travelling, you and I."

Tulan's eagle-spirit spreads its wings and flies up, up away. A true eagle of flesh and feathers would have pushed Tulan to the ground with the force of its talons, but he barely seems to notice his guide is gone.

Heart hammering, I take up the sheep bones and drop them one by one into the flames. There's a quick sizzling as clinging scraps of tendon and flesh blacken, charring. Smoke rakes the back of my throat. I close my eyes. To travel with my master, I must turn away from the world of men; I must forget it all – fire, warmth, talk, good meat and hot kumis, the touch of my mother, anger, joy, the smell of horses, Baba laughing. Everything. It is so hard to do.

At my side, I hear Shaman Tulan's deep, steady breathing. He is already gone, leaving his body a hollow shell, but in my mind I see Yan and Tela walking away from the fire, hand-in-hand, and again I taste the sourness of jealousy. It's like bad milk.

I push it all away. To journey to the World Above, I must

think of nothing. I must be as nothing, just as I have to do when I wish to be hidden.

I feel a swift tug deep in my belly and stare at the waving bulrushes, at the sunlight on the waters: I am here, but not here. At last, at last – I am leaving my body, leaving it behind like an old jacket crumpled on the ground.

I fly free.

I'm astride my spirit-horse, up in the World Above. Tulan rides at my side. His eagle-guide swoops above us in the unstained sky. My wolf runs ahead, a swift shadow half hidden by swaying grass. Cold fear slips through me. Straying from the body for too long is dangerous, even for a shaman. All worlds touch: the worlds of spirit, the world of men – and Shaman Tulan is old. Of late, he has been out of his body more often than not. He is like a man in a boat trailing his fingers in the water, leaning further and further over the edge till he falls.

My spirit-horse rides faster, faster. Tulan keeps pace at my side. We leave the shimmering grasslands of the World Above far below, riding hard through clear blue sky.

Look down, Shaman Tulan says, and the grasslands of the World Above fade; now we are soaring high above our own camp, high over the earth, watching sheep moving like small tufts of grey cloud down among the pine trees. Back by the tents, our horses are shifting where they stand, uneasy, ready to run. I see my horse Shadow at the herd's edge, watching for danger.

Far to the west, a line of laden horse-folk edges onward,

bound for Constantinople, where Mama was born, or perhaps even Rome. Each beast is no larger than my little finger from this great height. There are camels, too, and wagons, and folk on foot trailing like beetles. One of them is a wicked man: his spirit-horse burns white-hot with rage that never fades.

Looking east, I glimpse the pale walls and seething streets of Samarkand, and a few days' ride further on a tangled splash of green: some trading post or other. It's like a foal birthed by the great city, left behind.

Watch, Tulan tells me. *They are coming home.*

Higher and higher we rise, Shaman Tulan and I, circling above the mountains. Now I see the horses: first, a creamy cloud of dust moving swift from the east. Not a wild herd but men, riding. Their spirit-horses shimmer like sunlight glancing off the lake. Fear. Battle-thirst. Men who want to fight. Our men. Even from this height I see how Kul sits in the saddle with a slump, how Baba is keeping back from the front, allowing Uncle Taspar to be first. The men are riding back to camp early, the trade roads abandoned. What has happened?

I look down again; my wolf runs at my side, treading the sky with his black, ragged paws. Tulan's eagle swoops down and lands upon his shoulder once more.

Why have the menfolk left the roads? Tulan asks. *We had not thought to see them again till the birth of a new moon.*

Tulan's eagle-guide answers: *They have heard whispers of death and battle to come. The Empress of the T'ang seeks to destroy the Tribes and rule the roads with her own might.*

Tulan shakes his head. *There was a time when the T'ang trembled in fear at the sound of galloping horses. What is to be done?*

There will be a Gathering of the Tribes, my wolf says. *Meet where the Great River comes down from the mountains and greets the plain in the shadow of Claw Rock. Together, the Tribes will choose a path. But you must beware.*

And the world of men fades around us; we are back in the World Above, galloping across the golden grasslands. I hear it again. Drumming hoofbeats, the screaming of horses and men alike. The thin lonely wail of a child. The dream unfolds before my eyes, here in the World Above, as if Shaman Tulan and I are watching a children's game of wooden dolls. It is my dream, the warning, and the dolls are real people dying on the ground without help or the rites of passing.

Watch, Tulan tells me. *Wait.*

The din of battle fades. It is only Shaman Tulan and I in the World Above, riding our spirit-horses across a plain of wind-rippled golden grass.

Tulan's eagle-guide is nowhere to be seen now, but my wolf comes leaping forward out of the grass till he stands before us.

Well? Tulan asks him. *I grow tired. Speak, friend. How can we stop this coming to pass?*

Our fate lies in Asena's hands, says my wolf. And he is gone.

So there you have it, Tulan says, and I feel the warmth of his smile. *The task is yours, Shaman Asena. You will save us from the T'ang.*

No! I cry out. *I can't do it alone. I am not ready to look after our people without you, and this is even worse. I can't manage a – a* war—

Shaman Tulan smiles again. *Many long years I have walked the earth, my wolf-girl, and I bargained with the spirits for another handful to see you grow to be a shaman. You are the most powerful of our kind in five generations, and I am so proud of you that I could weep. Yet I must stay no longer. Take the buckskin from around my shoulders. It is yours now.* Tulan's spirit-horse rears on her hindlegs, eager to be away.

Tulan is going. He is leaving me. I reach out to hold him back but it's no use. *Be ready*, he says, clasping my hand one last time. *Your powers will remain strong only if you live by truth alone. Heed your wolf or lose him. Trust him. Never forget: the spirits only guide those willing to be led.*

I cannot stop him. I can do nothing but watch in horror as my old friend rides away across the whispering, shifting grasslands of the World Above, leaving me with the burden of a prophecy: *Our fate lies in Asena's hands. You will save us from the T'ang.* What am I to do? I must return to camp alone.

I sit upright, back at the fireside, back in the world of men. The light hurts my eyes; it glitters across the lake. A wind has got up, singing through the mulberry trees above my head.

The waters are shifting. The sound of laughter and voices drifts from camp, the clang of a dropped pot.

I kneel at Tulan's side. No longer sitting up, he has slumped to the ground. His face is pale and bloodless; his eyes are closed. I see the thin blue veins on his eyelids. I know he is dead. There is no breath in his body. I help him to lie down. I feel numb, as if I've been swimming in icy water. The T'ang are coming to destroy the Tribes and I am the one to stop them.

I cannot do it.

"Tulan." I clutch his hand, wildly hoping that he is not really dead, that this burden is not mine to bear alone. But he is cold to the touch already, like a stone pulled from the bottom of a river. Tears slide hot and fierce down my face.

Back at camp, someone cries out for more tea. I hear Aunt Zaka saying, "Get it yourself, slug."

He has left me at last. My old friend, my teacher. He is gone.

How can anyone drink tea while Tulan lies here cold? The cruelty of it snatches the breath from my lungs: tonight his place by our hearth will be empty and we shall all eat our meat without him.

I cannot lift him alone. I will have to get help. I must give Tulan the death-rites or else his souls will not find their next home, and he will wander.

Take the buckskin from around my shoulders, he had said. I obey, easing the cloak out from beneath his body. The buckskin is heavy and its fringed edges trail between my fingers.

I close my eyes and in my mind I see Shaman Tulan dancing, beating his drum, the cloak spinning out around him,
rising and falling like the wings of Raven, the first shaman.
My tears make dark splashes on the deer-hide. I have no
choice: the buckskin cloak is mine to wear. I pull it on, feeling its weight. It smells of thyme, burnt juniper. Even with
the fire's heat and the cloak, I am cold.

Wait. What's that sound? It's like drumbeats. Placing one
hand flat on the ground, I feel the earth trembling. Horses. I
hear as keen and sharp as a wolf. The men *are* coming home.
Baba is riding home and how I long to see him. But dread
crushes the spark of joy. So it begins. The T'ang are coming;
there is to be a battle, which I am somehow to prevent.

How?

I stare at Tulan's body. He looks so small and frail. He
cannot help me now.

I am shaman. I must find the strength to guide the spirits
of my people. I must do what I was born to do. Tears stream
down my face, and the truth is they are not only for my dear
wise Tulan, but for the unknown boy I will never love, the
children I will never bear him. The life I want that will never
be mine.

4

Swiftarrow
Samarkand, several days later

Swiftarrow sat in a shadowy alleyway between an old woman selling leather purses and a man charring mutton over a fire in an iron bowl. They did not see him and neither did anyone else in the surging crowd: sun-burnt, wind-reddened men with dirty cloaks that once were bright-dyed, now faded with the desert sun, women in dark robes with faces like rock shaped by the harsh, hot wind, and scruffy children who ran and shrieked.

Swiftarrow's mouth filled with spit at the meat's rich fatty smell: he'd had his first taste of dried salt pork on the roads, and he knew the pickled cabbage and mushroomy broths Hano served at home in the Forbidden Garden would never truly fill his belly again. He fought off a burst of guilt: one of his earliest memories was watching Brother Red Falcon take great care to lift a drowning worm from a puddle in the Alley of the Jingling Harness, just after his mother had died.

Red Falcon was the ninth son of a powerful lord from the south, but he was also Shaolin. To rescue the worm he had crouched so low that the ragged edge of his robe was soaked in muddy water.

Why do you do that? It's just a worm, Swiftarrow had asked. He remembered thinking, *How can a worm be saved from death and not our mother?*

Red Falcon had smiled, his scarred face bright with kindness as he patted Swiftarrow's shoulder. *All life is sacred, child – even the worms. Come.* He had taken him to the pastry-seller for honeyed plums, which to this day Swiftarrow could never taste without the ache of grief for his mother.

Frowning, he leaned back against the wall, watching blue smoke bloom from the mutton-seller's fire. *If all life is sacred, then why am I here? If I lead General Li to the Horse Tribes, people will die. If I take a recruit for our temple, they too will be trained to steal secrets from traitors and deliver them to death just as I have done.*

But there was White Swan, captive in the house of Golden Butterflies. In truth, his sister was a hostage, and Swiftarrow had no choice.

Reaching into his tunic, he touched the silver phial of sleeping-draught hanging around his neck. Would he need it, or would the chosen victim come without a struggle?

Ensure no one ever pays heed to you, Autumn Moon had told him. *Be as a shadow; be nothing. Watch the market places: that shall be where you find the right kind of folk – thieves, pickpockets – those who know how to go unnoticed.* Swiftarrow stared down at his dust-pale hands. He had seen thieves in Samarkand, but they were just scrawny, scampering children made fearless by hunger. They darted about the market places and through the tangle of alleyways like young carp in a pool, snatching dried figs here, a handful of spices there.

How can I return to the Empress with such a prize? She hardly sent me across the desert for brats like those: Chang'an is full of them already. She wants someone different. She wants someone with the blood of the Tribes.

Swiftarrow got to his feet and climbed the wall, swift and silent as a falling leaf. It was easier to watch folk from the rooftops, away from the stench and crush below. Breathing easier, he walked on, making neat jumps from one rooftop to the next.

One, two, three… Leaving his doubts behind, Swiftarrow began to count, leaping and landing in a crouch on one dusty rooftop after another. The pepper-market was long behind him now; the streets below were wider, less crowded. Camels and mules lumbered past, laden with bundles.

I must be near one of the city gates. Swiftarrow glanced up at the sun; it was setting before his eyes, a ball of red fire sinking lower over the jumble of pale rooftops and dusty courtyards half hidden by cook-fire smoke. *The west wall.* Running towards the dying sun, Swiftarrow landed at last on the rooftop of a silk warehouse. The crowd thickened again here: traders bustled outside among the throng of camels. An old woman selling reed-woven baskets sat on the rim of a fountain; she reached back with one hand and let her crooked brown fingers trail in the water. When Swiftarrow looked straight down, he saw two men lounging by a pile of sack-wrapped silk bales, leaning against the wall of the warehouse. They were playing knuckle stones with sheeps' teeth, not real knucklebones; the teeth clicked together softly.

Merchants from the east, selling silk to merchants from the west, he thought. *All the way to barbarian cities, where folk are double the height of real men and have hair the colour of fire.*

He could hear horses now – not far away, either: that strange, whinnying cry. Swiftarrow frowned again, glancing down at the street below. *No horses here, only camels.* Rising to his feet, he ran across the rooftop and looked down on the crumbling western city wall of Samarkand. He stopped and stared. Beyond the wall, out in the open, a rash of deer-hide tents clustered around a group of people sitting by a fire, thumb-sized from so far off. Only men, though: no women. Men with long plaited hair, rough cloaks, leggings that fitted close. Barbarian clothes, like those worn by General Li's half-blood Horse Tribers lighting fires in the courtyard of that trader-inn.

My mother's brethren: the Tribes.

Swiftarrow could not look away. A small gaggle of men had left the fire's warmth, leading horses to a stream. In the dying light, the water shone like the blade of a knife. The men walked with a bow-legged gait: they were in the saddle more often than on their feet.

Swiftarrow froze. He closed his eyes, hearing again his mother's last words: *My spirit runs free like a horse, dear ones, and so do yours. Even within a locked room, you shall be free, my loves. Do not forget.* He remembered waiting at the deathbed, White Swan standing at his side, gripping his hand so tight that her fingers left red burning marks.

Forget Mother: she's dead, Swiftarrow told himself. *You may have the blood of the Tribes, but you're T'ang and you are also Shaolin.*

Yet he could not help staring at the camp beyond the wall.

If Mother were not dead, I would be like them. I would be free.

The horses weren't roped: they just followed the men. It was as if they spoke to one another without words. It was clear these people never slid from the saddle or commanded a horse to walk on, only to find the beast refused to move. *They treat the horses as kin,* Swiftarrow thought, *all walking together down to the water at sunset like old friends looking for a good tavern.* He swallowed another swift, sharp pang of longing that dug into his belly like a knife. *Barbarians. They've never even been near a bath-house.* He turned to look at the tents, low and humped close to the ground. *How do they wash?* And, as he watched, someone stepped out of the nearest tent.

It was a girl, tall and long-limbed. Black hair hung in two plaits over her shoulders, all the way down to her waist. She moved like a cat: swift, neat, wasting no effort. What was she wearing? Some kind of fringed cloak? *I bet the barbarians keep their women as slaves.* Swiftarrow thought of his temple-sister Autumn Moon, mistress of the Forbidden Garden, equal to any of the brothers. The girl drew her cloak tighter; she was heading for the camp where, judging by the laughter and raised voices, the gathered men were sharing a skinful of something fiery.

Most likely they've brought her along to cook and wash for them all.

But the girl did not stop when she reached the campfire.

She walked straight past the men, heading for the wall, for the West Gate of Samarkand, and not one of them turned his head to look at her. Swiftarrow crouched on his rooftop, still as a stone, scarcely able to believe it.

She was like him. The girl had simply made sure that she was not seen.

"You," Swiftarrow said. He would not fail after all. "It's you."

Now he was a hunter: now there was prey.

5

Asena
Samarkand

Someone is following me. I feel their gaze hot on the back of my neck. They've been watching me since before I came into the pepper-market, but each time I turn around, I see nothing but the heaving crowd. The air's heavy with the kick of spices and market-men calling; it makes my head spin. I wish I'd not left camp now. No one saw me go, either. I wish they had. I ought to have told them where I was bound, but I didn't know then. I was just thirsty for the city, longing to wander alone down shaded alleyways that wind about on themselves, to forget who I am, my grief, my burden.

Shemi will be riled with me for going without him. At first, he was foolish with pride at being asked along to the Gathering but this morning as we scrubbed out last night's stew-pots with mulberry sticks, he whispered to me, "I wish we'd been left behind with Yan and the others. It'll be all the worst jobs for us till we get home." For once, he was right.

I stop again, leaning against a stall where a fat woman sells chipped pots and rolls of badly cured leather and peppercorns from great wooden tubs. The stink of pepper-dust and rotting hide makes my eyes water. I wipe them with the back of one hand, breathing fast. I don't like this. I don't like being watched.

The stallholder's arguing with a scrawny, sweat-stained man over something; they're not of the Tribes so I can't follow their speech. Either way, they pay no mind to me.

Will they help if I cry out, these strangers?

I gaze at the crowd seething through the market; sweat slides down my face, down the back of my neck, even though there's no heat left in the sun. Soon it will be night. If there *is* someone following me, I'll seek him out now and ask what he means by trailing me all the way from the West Gate. I must have been mistaken for some other girl. That's it.

The crowd shifts as folk surge about. As always when I am among wall-dwellers, I feel this cold shiver of disgust, for they are not like us. Wall-dwellers have no spirit-horses and keep their souls locked within their bodies, tight and secret. I shudder. It is just as if they had no eyes, noses or mouths, and their faces were smooth and round like eggs. Mama was born a wall-dweller, but her spirit-horse is free now she lives among the Tribes.

The prickling down the back of my neck grows worse: I'm still being watched, and the watcher's closer. I know it.

Maybe Shemi got tired of listening to the men telling wild tales and he's trailing me in jest. But if that were so, I should see his spirit-horse flickering above the crowd, tail flicking, head tossing – and I do not.

It must be a stranger who follows me. I lean back against the post again, trying to pick him out from the crowd. So many faces. So many different voices. How can these folk live in such a way? Blood pounds in my ears; my heart's racing. I'm trapped here among all these people with no horse beneath me, no Shadow to take me galloping far from danger. I'm like a goose fallen out of the sky, clumsy on the ground.

A hollow-eyed trader shouts and curses as he tries to push his cart through the throng— *There* – right behind him is a man clad all in black, watching me.

He comes closer, and *wait*—

The watcher shifts, hidden within the crowd once more, melting away like a bowlful of curds left out in the sun. Relief washes through me. Have I imagined it? *Foolish girl*, I tell myself. *Why would any stranger be following you?*

My heart's still racing.

I must get back to Baba and the others: they'll miss me before long. I may be shaman, but someone must feed them. It makes me wonder why the men do not all starve when they go trading, and without my help Shemi is about as much use as—

Mother Earth save me.

I see a flash of darkness among the stream of people.

The watcher is no more than a spit away. *How did that happen? Where did he go?* He moves so light and quick. No one else in the crowd pays any mind at all. No one need step from his path; no one shoulders him aside. The stranger moves like smoke on the wind, hardly here at all, yet the heat of his gaze burns my skin. I stand fear-frozen, like a mouse before a snake.

If I don't get away from here, he will catch me: I'm sure of it. No time to think. The crowd closes around me as I sprint west, heading for the city walls and our camp. I wish I were in the saddle with nothing but the open sky before me. I glance behind and catch a glimpse of black. The stranger is still behind, still following.

Who is he? What does he want with me?

If I lag too much, I'll find out and I don't wish to. I run so fast my heart's bursting; sweat pours down the back of my neck, down my face, into my eyes so that I can scarcely see. The ground is hard beneath my bare feet. I duck past a camel laden with rolled-up carpets; I weave through the endless crowd.

The great crumbling west wall rises up before me. Two guards lounge on either side of the gate, gazing idly at the crowd. One is nearly asleep, tea-flask held loose in one hand.

What's that?

Here's a hand, fingers closing around my arm. *The stranger.* I'm caught. I gasp; his touch is red-hot. I can't see his face for he is masked, a black silken scarf covering nose and mouth rippling like water as he breathes. Dark eyes burn into me, flecked with green like deep water.

And, just for a heartbeat, I see a spirit-horse shimmering above his left shoulder. Now it's gone.

Who are you? The world slows down as if we are swimming in honey. I reach up and snatch the mask from his face, a scrap of black silk; quick as thought, he grabs my wrist – another burning jolt – and the sight of him tears the breath from my lungs. Green slanted eyes, skin burnt gold by the desert's heat, hair stripped of its deep black by the sun; it is fire-coloured in places: dark red, golden, too. The clamour and bright jumble of Samarkand fades, blurring.

It is just me and this boy staring speechless at one another as if we have slipped from the world of men altogether.

What am I doing? The boy raises his other hand as if to strike me, and white-hot fear sears through my body.

Run, you fool of a girl. Run.

I am not here. You can't catch me.

If I think of nothing, there is no one to catch, for I become nothing. I am but a shadow, a ghost, fading away. Crying out, I wheel about, wrenching myself from the stranger's grasp. I know not where this strength comes from and I care even less.

The stranger is gone. The whisper of his curse hangs on the air a moment and fades to silence.

The guards barely look up as I reach the gate. I'm just a girl, beneath their concern.

"Let me out!" I fight to keep my voice steady. I don't want to stir them up, though it looks as if it would take nothing less than an earthquake.

They swing the gate open for me and I pass by, trying not to shake. My wrist still burns where the boy touched me, as if I leaned too close to the fire and was licked by a flame. But my skin is clear and smooth – untouched.

Baba has spotted me already – a thousand curses. I ought to have slipped back into camp without being seen. He breaks away from the fire, loping towards me. The sharp reek of kumis hangs on the air, mingling with the smell of horses, warm and comforting.

The stranger had a spirit-horse – it was weak, hardly even there at all, twisted and faded by wickedness. Who is he? Why was he following me? Some wrongdoer driven away from his tribe, wits scattered with wandering alone? I've heard that can happen. He must be mad. Why else would a boy with a face like that be following *me*?

"Asena." Baba reaches me, resting one hand on my shoulder, pulling me close. He folds me in his arms. His hair is stiff, windblown, blacker than scorched grass. His striped wool jacket is warm with the scent of smoke, spices and pepper-oil: shadows of the trade roads. "Where have you been? Is something wrong?" He shakes his head. "My love, listen: you are our shaman. You cannot just wander the streets of Samarkand alone. If anything were to happen—"

"Well, nothing did." The lie slips out, my voice sharp. "Can I not be alone for a single afternoon?"

Baba stares at me, still shaking his head. "Asena, I know you are grieving for our old friend; we all are, but—"

I turn and walk away, back to camp, leaving him staring after me, half angry, half bemused. I know he is wishing that the women and brats had come with us after all and that Mama were here to unpick the mysteries of my female heart. I'm not going to tell him anything. Why should I? I'm not even sure what happened myself. My kinsmen are burning for a fight. If I tell them a boy followed me, they will chase him through the streets of Samarkand; they might even kill him. I've heard enough such idiotic tales; I know the terrible, bloody things men do if the honour of a tribeswoman has been insulted. I'll keep this to myself.

Foolish, says my wolf-guide, prowling out of nowhere.

For the first time in my life, I ignore him, and when I next look, he is gone. If I told Baba the truth, he would never let me out of his sight again. Yet another price I pay for being shaman: I am forever overwatched. In my mind, I hear Shaman Tulan's last words to me: *Your powers will remain strong only if you live by truth alone. Heed your wolf or lose him. Trust him. Never forget: the spirits only guide those willing to be led.* Well, maybe I want to carve out my own path for once. It was only a small lie. I'm not going to turn some ragged boy over to my battle-hungry kinsmen just because he followed me in Samarkand. What can he have to do with the T'ang, with this army I am supposed to send running back to the east, as if I might have the strength to dam a flooding river with my little finger?

My wolf will be back.

I can't help looking over my shoulder, back at the crumbling walls of Samarkand. Shall I catch another glimpse of the boy? Would he follow me here? Who was he?

A ball of fear unfolds within me like the petals of a frozen flower, but with it a small, bright flame of excitement.

6

Swiftarrow

Swiftarrow crouched in the dark. Alone, he watched. The Horse Tribers were eating cooked meat – he could smell the richness of it; his belly was hollow like a rotten nut. He looked down at his hand again, staring at the palm. He couldn't help it. He still felt the burning jolt from when he'd grabbed her wrist, as if a knot of fire had passed from her body into his. Even now, he expected to see the skin puckered and seared, but of course it was not.

He had let her go. It had been like snatching a burning branch from the fire. She had torn the mask from his face and looked straight through him, right into his mind, or that was how it felt. Why? She was not even pretty. It was not as if he could claim to have been struck senseless by her beauty. He had just been outwitted by a lanky, dust-grimed barbarian girl and that was all.

By the goddess of the moon, what is wrong with you?

Swiftarrow asked himself. Autumn Moon would be so ashamed if she knew how easily he'd failed. But there was no use in mourning over the past. *I will get her, sooner or later.*

Swiftarrow turned his attention back to the Horse Tribe camp. Here she was now, handing around a bowl, which the men dipped their food into. The girl passed her bowl to the smallest of the men – perhaps just a boy – and left the campfire, walking towards the nearest tent. Now she was less than a handful of paces from where he watched, hidden among a dark tangle of mulberry trees. He could smell the smoke in her hair, in her worn homespun jacket and trousers. Suddenly his prey stopped, very still, just like a cat before it leaps on a mouse. Clouds shifted in the night sky, and her face was lit up by the moon: long dark eyes, mouth set firm. Listening, waiting.

You know, he thought. *You know I am watching, but I have been playing this game for longer than you.* He would get her in the end. The first person ever to have escaped him, and she was not even Shaolin. He pushed away the white-hot rage that had crashed through him as she'd slipped from his grasp. *Be calm or you will fail again.*

The girl ducked into a tent and came out a few moments later holding a flask. She pulled out the stopper with one firm twist and dipped her finger inside.

"My gift to you, the spirits." Her voice was low, quiet. She flicked the pale liquid to each of the four directions. A barbarian superstition: Swiftarrow had seen General Li's Horse Tribers do the same.

Swiftarrow watched her walk back to the campfire and pass the flask to a man sitting a little apart from the others. He was rangy and long-legged, too. Her father? An older brother? Certainly a kinsman. The man pulled her close, kissing the side of her head. She said something Swiftarrow could not hear and walked off to a tent on the far side of the campfire. A puddle of light spilled out as the girl opened the flap, disappearing as she closed it behind her.

Silently, Swiftarrow got to his feet, moving closer to the fire. She could wait. He had chosen his prey, but for now, he would listen.

"...that's the trouble with womenfolk, brother," a fat-bellied man said, taking a long draught from his flask. "Most often they make no sense at all, so do not worry your head about it. Best to leave the managing of daughters to their mothers."

The man who had kissed the girl shook his head. "But her mother is not here, Taspar, is she?"

So he *was* her father. Swiftarrow wondered what she was thinking, shut away in her tent. Was she afraid? She had not seemed it, tearing away his mask, staring him in the face without a shadow of fear in her eyes. *Don't think about her father and mother or you won't be able to do it. You have a sister, and she will die if you fail in this. If the Empress wants a barbarian Shaolin toy, she must have one.*

The girl's father sighed. "One more moon to Claw Rock. A moon at the Gathering. A moon to ride home, and after that I can ask the advice of her mother again, but not before."

"A moon to journey home?" muttered one of the other men. "Not if we don't ride out to fight the T'ang first, Istemi."

And Swiftarrow smiled in the darkness. General Li had not been far wrong, after all: the Tribes were leaving their scattered grazing lands and clustering together, ready for the general's legion to destroy them. So it was to be a gathering at Claw Rock, wherever that was. His barbarian girl would have to wait before he took her captive: first she and her kin would lead him to their nest of rebels. How would that pig-faced lout General Li swallow the news? *I shall deliver him an ambush, and then take my prisoner.*

A day later, Swiftarrow returned to his general. Outside the inn, he slid from the saddle in the early-evening cool, aching all over. Since he had been gone, the leaves had burst from their buds, filling the night with a rich green scent that quickened his blood. Cursing softly, he rubbed at his legs. *Six days in Samarkand and already my body protests at a day's ride.* What he would not give now for a steaming pool of warm water and a girl to knead the pain from his shoulders. The air was blue with campfire smoke and ringing with a muddle of voices speaking in both Horse Tribe and T'ang: General Li and his men. Patting the mare's flank, Swiftarrow beckoned to one of the ragged boys playing by the gate, digging into his belt-bag for a coin.

"You – give the beast food and water, and brush her down."

The brat's eyes widened at the sight of the coin, snatching

it from Swiftarrow's outstretched hand. His fingers were dry and skinny like little twigs. *I could have been like that but for the temple,* Swiftarrow thought, watching the boy lead his horse away into the inner courtyard. Soon he would have to trade the beast for another one of those accursed camels to make the desert-crossing – but not yet. Not yet.

We have a task to do first.

He found General Li sitting by the fountain, sharing a flask of rice wine with the aristocratic young conscript.

"No new Shaolin? You failed, then, boy." General Li lounged back against the fountain, taking a swig from the flask, one hand resting against his great belly. "What will your master say about that, eh?" He smiled, showing teeth like yellow pearls. "Perhaps now Her Imperial Highness will trust in her old faithful army again and forget this woman-ish infatuation with holy men who fight and sneak about like rats."

Swiftarrow shrugged.

"Show some respect to your betters!" roared the general, letting forth a cloud of wine-sour breath. The young aristo-crat stared goggle-eyed at Swiftarrow's want of conduct. General Li lurched to his feet, hand raised and ready to strike.

Quicker than thought, Swiftarrow stepped backwards, out of reach. Would the old toad never learn? "Do you wish to know where the barbarians are gathering, or not?"

General Li sank back into his seat, wine-reddened eyes

narrowing. Swiftarrow knew that in his mind the general saw a triumphant return to Chang'an, kneeling before the Empress, scattered with peach petals.

"Speak then, half-breed." He spat on the ground.

Call me what you like, Swiftarrow thought; *you know I hold the winning dice.*

7

Asena
Claw Rock, one moon later

I run so fast my chest is going to burst open like a rotten plum, but he's still behind me. I hear the beating of his heart, louder than Shaman Tulan's drum when we converse with the spirits. Faceless people crowd in, blocking my path; shadows loom overhead. A hand grasps me tight; long fingers close around my arm. I'm caught; I'm caught—

The dream shifts.

I lie on hard ground, sightless, the left side of my body burning in pain. I feel the pain even though I know I am only dreaming: searing hot, aching, sucking the breath from my lungs. I open my eyes and here he is, leaning over me. Green eyes, gold-burnt hair hanging over his face. The stranger has caught up with me at last. He speaks but I don't understand the words. This time, I'm not afraid. He reaches out; with a light warm touch he moves a tangled hank of hair away from my face—

I wake, gasping. I'm so cold: I must have thrown off my

blanket. Who is he? What are the spirits trying to tell me now? That the strange boy is not a threat but a saviour? I sit up, clutching the blanket about my shoulders, taking long, steady breaths. Everyone around me is still sleeping: Baba, Uncle Taspar, Shemi and the other men. Baba's cousin Kul lies on his back, snoring. I shiver; when I close my eyes, still I see the boy's face, burnt into my mind.

Who are you?

The campfire smoulders, and the white mountain-tops glow in the moonlight. Far off, where land meets sky, I can just make out the curved ridge of Claw Rock, bright with snow. The air is thinner up here after ten days' hard uphill trekking. It's not so easy to breathe and my chest feels tight. Samarkand's a long way behind us, but each night I have the same dream. I would give anything to see Shaman Tulan now. Who else could I tell about it? Baba? Shall I? But he is sorrowing for Mama and troubled in his heart. He does not want to die fighting the T'ang without seeing her again. He worries for my safety as it is. I can't add to his fears by telling of strange, feverish dreams.

Hunched in my blanket, alone among sleepers, I stare at the campfire, watching dark red clots of smouldering wood. The same questions wheel about in my mind: why did the boy follow me? His spirit-horse was so faint I could hardly see it: I've never seen one so weak and shadowy. Wouldn't it take many long years to cripple your soul so terribly? Years of lying and selfishness? Or just one dreadful crime, like taking a life. Could he be a murderer? What if he needs the help of a shaman for some other reason – grief, perhaps? I wear the buckskin cloak, after all: he must know what I am. Yet if I dream of him watching over me with such tenderness, then he must mean no harm. I did right not to tell Baba I was followed. I'm sure of it.

Night upon night, I have prayed for my wolf-guide to come slinking out of the darkness and take me soaring to the World Above, seeking answers. But he does not come. Why are my powers fading? If the boy means nothing but good, my lie hasn't caused any harm. Was such a small untruth enough to send away my wolf-guide for ever? I curl up again, pulling the blanket up over my head, burying my face in the sheepskin bedroll. I breathe in the smell of woodsmoke, the bone-cold night air, waiting for sleep to come. But whenever I close my eyes, I see a black-clad stranger pushing through a crowd of faceless people. I want to see the boy again, and maybe my wolf-guide knows. Maybe this is why he has left me.

My wish is still the same.

Night fades into day; daylight pours into the darkness, swimming across the sky from the east. With each day, the curved ridge of Claw Rock has grown nearer, rising up head and shoulders above the rest of the mountains like an older brother. Now we're close enough to catch sight of the great peak through the branches wherever the trees thin. Still we ride, spirit-horses flickering above us like new flames, almost too quick and lithe for the eye to catch hold of. Despite my night-time fears, the thrill of it simmers within me: never before have I been among so many of my own tribe. Uncle Taspar says there will be horse-racing, dancing, games.

I'm in the lead with Baba and Shemi behind me, and I know we're close: I sense the heat of many spirit-horses. The air thrums with laughter, anger, idle chat, all drifting on the wind but heard only by me. I think I can even smell wood-smoke: it's got a sharper kick to it than the sheep's dung fires we burn at home.

At last, the trees begin to thin properly and the hillside sweeps out below, darkened in patches with stands of walnut, mulberry, tall green spears of larch. It tumbles down towards a great bowl of a valley shot through by a river. The mountains rise again, white and merciless, Claw Rock snatching at the sky dead ahead of us. But that's not what steals my breath.

The valley seethes with people: from this height they look like ants I once saw crawling over a sheep's skull. Tents are scattered everywhere; some in clusters, some alone. I see poles with pennants of silk flapping: silk from the trade roads, silk from the east. There are more fires than I can count; smoke rises, dragged sideways by the wind. On the riverbank, a great blaze bigger than any other sends coils of smoke up to the World Above.

"The talk-fire," Baba says, riding up alongside me. He takes my hand and squeezes it. "It's where we shall meet with the elders, and you will take your place alongside the shamans."

I squeeze his hand back, silently. I fight a gathering sense of unease: what kind of shaman am I, who cannot even summon her own wolf-guide? And anyhow, I don't know what I will say when we meet by this talk-fire. There must be other shamans here wiser than I. I pray they will know the meaning of my wolf's message:

Our fate lies in Asena's hands.

In my mind, I hear Tulan's words to me again: *The task is yours, Shaman Asena. You will save us from the T'ang.*

What will all these wise elders say when I speak of this? I am just a scrawny girl wearing the cloak of her dead master. They'll laugh in my face.

And when I look back at the men of my own tribe, I shudder, for all of them – even Shemi – have a faraway, blank look in their eyes. Their spirit-horses toss their manes, paw at the air with their hooves. I've seen this look before, three winters ago when all the men rode out to fight another tribe over horse-stealing. Not all came back, of course, but that never stops them. It is the look of men thirsting to fight, craving to redeem their honour.

I think of my dream again: people lying dead on the ground, cries of the wounded. Afraid, I stare down the path at the starflower vines hanging tangled from dark branches. My wolf-guide slinks from the shadows and my heart thuds. At last. Oh, at last. But he is faint, shadowy. It is as if I look at him through clouds of thick smoke. I hear his voice in my mind, but quietly:

When will you act, Asena?

When I next look, he is gone. Relief washes through me, mingled with fear as questions race through my mind like a herd of galloping horses. I don't understand what he means, what I am to do. Why does he look so faded? Why won't he come when I call? Uncle Taspar is already pushing on ahead. Baba rides past, laying a hand on my shoulder.

"Come, dear one. It's time we joined the Gathering."

"I'm coming," I say. Baba gives me a long look, raising an eyebrow at the hard edge to my voice. It is the closest he will get to a rebuke. If Baba knew what I know, he would understand. The Tribes have gathered from north, south, east and west. The valley swarms with people and horses. What if the Tribes decide to fight, and all the men ride off to battle the T'ang? They need a shaman to guide their spirits. They need me. If they knew I couldn't even summon my own wolf-guide, fear would grip their hearts.

It's past noon and the sun is beating down on us, adding to the heat kicked out by the talk-fire. Sweat slides down my back in cool trickles. The talking will soon begin. I sit close by Baba and Taspar, watching people's souls. Shemi wanted to come with us, but Taspar said there was work enough with tents to put up, fire-pits to dig. I could see it cost Taspar dear to bring me: to him, I am still just the girl-child of his younger brother, not a shaman at all.

Everywhere I look, spirit-horses flicker, rearing up on their hindlegs, shining like silver flames. We are here with the tribal elders to speak of the T'ang, and it's clear most folk burn with the desire to fight the Empress's greed in the old Tribe way: with a bow and death-headed arrows, from the back of a galloping horse. I don't just see spirit-horses, either: there's a deer-spirit by that grey-haired man, a hawk across the fire, another wolf like mine, a hound. For the first time since Shaman Tulan went to the World Below, I am in the company of other shamans.

A chief with hair woven in plaits speaks out, holding up one hand for quiet. "What will befall the Tribes if we allow the T'ang to rule the Roads? Not only will there be taxes; it is but another way for the Empire to spread like a stain across our land."

A shout goes up, rippling through the gathered crowd, and the spirit-horses burn so bright I blink. "Ay, ay!" men call. "Kotan of the South speaks truth – we must fight!"

"Fighting is no use. How can we hope to win?" My voice rings out, far louder than I'd meant. A thick, unfriendly silence falls around the talk-fire. Everyone is looking at me, a skinny girl wrapped in the deer-hide cloak of a shaman.

Taspar curses quietly. Baba lays one hand over mine. The dry warmth of his touch lends me courage.

Now I have begun, I may as well finish. I draw in a deep breath, straightening my back, returning the stares. "I had a dream—"

My voice is drowned by a roar of jeering and mocking laughter: "What shall we do then, wench?" … "Who is this girl, anyhow?" … "Why should we pay her any heed?" …

"Go scrub the cook-pots and leave this talk to the men."

"Leave my daughter be." Baba speaks softly, but folk seem to listen all the same, and they fall quiet.

"Rein the girl in, then – who is she to speak out at our talk-fire?" calls Kotan of the South.

"She is one who deserves your respect, Kotan," Taspar replies. And I think, *So does this mean I now have yours, dear uncle?* The one called Kotan leaps to his feet, ready to fight, and so does my uncle. What have I started?

"Peace, brother," Baba says to Taspar, but he does not listen.

Everyone is staring: I wish I could sink into the ground.

The grey-haired shaman with the deer-spirit frowns, spitting. As I watch, he reaches into the leather bag at his waist and brings out a handful of something, casting it into the fire. A gust of flames boils up and everyone falls silent. Wordless, Taspar and Kotan both sit down again. I stare at the ground, head bowed.

"Speak not so to a shaman, Kotan of the South." The older man's voice is harsh, commanding. I don't like the way he is looking at me: it is not friendly. A chilly, unsettling thought slides into my mind: since Tulan died, I have not been in the presence of anyone able to see my souls. Why does this deer-shaman seem so – so *worried*? That's it: he looks worried. "Who are you, girl?" he says, never taking his eyes from me. "Who is your master?"

I swallow. My throat is dry. "I cannot say his name, for he is gone to the World Below, but the summer pastures of my tribe lie to the west of Samarkand, and his guide was an eagle."

The deer-shaman bows his head a moment. "I know of whom you speak. May your tribe take my sorrow at the passing of a great man." He sighs. "And dearly do I wish he were with us now, for your master held more power in his little fingernail than the rest of us put together. We are in need of one like him—" He breaks off and stares at me. No one speaks. All I hear is the fire crackling, distant shouting and laughter of children, and beyond that the hissing rush of the river.

Everyone stares but it is only I and the other shamans who see the old man's deer-guide break away from his side and run lightly through the air towards me, shimmering with reddish light. I can't breathe. I fight the urge to scramble to my feet and run, just to get away from the crowd, staring and wondering why this old man has chosen to single me out. The deer-guide gets almost close enough to touch, then shies away as if startled by a wolf in the forest at night, leaping back to the side of her shaman.

"Is that one you?" the deer-shaman says quietly, never taking his eyes off me. "There was a time when *your* power rivalled that of your master, wolf-girl. Am I right? And yet now—"

He knows. He knows I am losing my strength.

I am frozen with fear. "I – I don't—" I whisper.

The old man carries on talking as if I have not even spoken. "Wolf-shaman," he says, "before the sun sets come back to this fire. I will speak to you then." *Does he really know that my wolf-guide won't show himself to me? Oh, Mother Earth – I hope not.* Hot shame washes over me.

Baba turns sharply and looks at me, questioning. I shrug, trying to ignore the shiver of unease sliding down my back.

"This girl talks sense," the deer-shaman says, glaring at the gathering. "It's clear her mind is sharper than some of yours, hungry for honour and glory." He spits again. "And that," he goes on, "truly does not say much for you folk." No one speaks a word. I swallow a flash of anger. What is his meaning? If I am a fool, these people are even worse? And how is it that when a young girl speaks, it is only to be mocked, while everyone is silent and respectful for an old man? Everyone stares, cowering, and the deer-shaman smiles, mirthless. "Hear this: in the time of our fathers we Horse Tribes ruled the steppe, and the T'ang cowered behind their walls, afraid of us. But the Empire has grown in strength since those days: the Emperor may be all but dead, yet his wife is not. We would be fools to doubt the Empress's strength and the depth of her thirst for power just because she is not a man." He pauses, but no one says a word. His deer-guide shines bright at his shoulder, a steady silver glow. "And the girl is right: we may not win a fight, should it come to that."

More uneasy quiet, then a woman sitting near the back calls, "Time was, the Tribes brought terror to the T'ang; they lived in fear of us. Who's to say we can't strike them down once more?"

The deer-shaman shakes his head. "Look about your-selves," he says. "How many clans have sent men and women to this Gathering? All? Who could be so foolish as to think it? Is there anyone among us who has come from across the Great Desert?" His voice rings out, harsh and mocking. "What, none of our eastern cousins answered the call? Not one? Yet word was sent." He pauses, and again his gaze falls on me. "I dream of being watched. Always watched."

I suddenly feel cold, never mind the buckskin cloak and the fire's heat.

Folk are murmuring now, looking about, uneasy. But no-body stands up to say, *I come from the east. I come from across the Great Desert, in the lap of the T'ang.*

A man with a wind-reddened face stands up, raising one hand. He is wary: his spirit-horse shimmers, ears lying flat against her head. "Last summer, my brothers and I traded very far east, right to the rim of the desert. We heard whis-pers that men with the blood of the Horse Tribes fight in the Empress's army for coin. We heard that the grandchild of our last great leader camps in the very shadow of her palace, doing her bidding like a child."

Another low rumble of angry voices.

"What? Lord Ishbal has become the Empress's pet? Come, that can't be true."

"Believe what you like. I know what I heard: Ishbal is not loyal to the Tribes but to the T'ang. And he is not here, is he?"

"Traitors!" A woman calls. "We ought to hunt them down and cut their stinking throats!"

Wait. What was that? The sun has slid behind a cloud, and a chill settles. I saw a shadow where there should be none. Heart pounding, I stare at the crowd, at the gathered tribesfolk.

"What are we to do?" someone shouts. "Let the Empire crush us?"

Raised voices blur into one roar: "We fight!" … "No, we must send envoys, bargain with them!" … "Don't be a fool—"

I know now what I must do: I need to speak with the deer-shaman alone. I will tell him about my dream; perhaps together we can weave a plan that might save us. But what about the shadow-boy? It was only one afternoon in Samarkand, after all. Should I tell or not?

I see it again: a shadow, and the sun is still behind that cloud. Is this why I feel so cold? I blink, and catch a glimpse of a faded, ghostly spirit-horse. *Here he is,* a boy clad all in black like a shadow, scarf drawn across his face, as if thinking of him was an act of summoning. He's on the other side of the fire, crouching between a fat woman with wild, unbraided grey hair and a group of young men.

He has found me.

I look up, across the fire. It is just me and the boy again, as if everyone else has melted away. He is masked once more, but I can see his eyes are thirsting for something, full of anger. Then he looks at me and I catch a sense of such a great, aching loneliness it knocks the breath from my lungs.

I should denounce you, here before all of my people, trailing
and following me.

Instead, I run.

8

Swiftarrow

S

he saw me.

Drawing in a sharp breath, Swiftarrow watched the girl flee, black plaits snaking down her back as she ran, deer-skin cloak flying out behind her, wild and fast as a hawk. No one paid the slightest heed, not even the men she had been sitting with. Now she was lost among the throng. Once again, the sight of her had knocked the wits from his skull. *What is the matter with me?* Free of the crowd, away from the great fire and the rush of angry voices, Swiftarrow knew he must find his own peace again. The girl had seen him. Yes, she had skills – she saw what most people did not; she slid beneath the notice of others, becoming as nothing – but Swiftarrow had trained among the Shaolin since he was four summers old. *If an unschooled barbarian girl could spot me among a crowd, could escape me, I have strayed from the Way. My chi is weak. I must seek my path.*

71

There was no time to waste thinking about her.

As Swiftarrow ran through the camp, seeking a place among the dark tangle of trees where he could meditate, he shut out the sound of children laughing, calling to one another, crying out their swift, hot joy at being alive.

By morning, they will all be dead, he thought. *And I led their killers here.*

He pelted through the trees, bare feet hardly touching the forest floor, the thick carpet of pine needles left undisturbed. He could hear General Li's men now, the faint hissing of their campfires, someone laughing at a coarse joke. Most likely they were all sharpening their knives, fletching new arrows. He could not bear to be among them. Li and his raggle-taggle soldiers were thirsting for a fight after so long cooped up in that trader-inn outside Samarkand, and then the lung-bursting trek across the mountains, following the Horse Tribes' trail. They were ready for blood, ready to kill.

He stopped, breathing hard, crouching down by a pine tree. Whispering tales of treason to the Empress back in Chang'an was one matter; causing the ambush of a gathering of men, women and brats was quite another. Swiftarrow pushed back his hair again, letting out another sigh. There were so many of them: children running among the tents, women laughing, calling out to one another, men talking around that great fire.

The children were really no different from little Eighth Daughter at home in the temple – only less able to defend themselves, for they were not Shaolin. So many lives all to be ended when General Li and his men rode out. Was duty to the Empress worth so much killing? *Only a few more hours of life on this earth, they have,* he thought. *When the sun has risen, they will all be dead. Surely it cannot be right?* Swiftarrow cursed and spat on the ground. It was wrong, however he looked at it.

He pushed the thought from his mind. There was no choice. *White Swan's life rests on it,* he told himself. *You have your orders. Obey them and return to Chang'an.*

He leaned back against the pine tree, closing his eyes against the forest, closing his ears against the far-off hum of voices from the barbarian camp and the nearer sounds of General Li's men talking among each other, playing at Go, clicking the black and white stones into place on a grid scraped onto the back of a shield. Across the clearing, a deer ran, dappled, half hidden in shadow. Peace was near. But in the dark corners of Swiftarrow's mind, there waited a girl with long black eyes and a dirty deer-hide cloak who rode lighter than a leaf on the wind.

Swiftarrow would be sorry to ruin her life, he knew. Before peace came at last, he thought: *Forgive me—* He did not even know her name.

Before the sun was down, she would be his captive.

9

Asena

Scarcely thinking, I run through the camp, past the throng of tents – more than I have ever seen in one spot – past the women and girls brewing tea outside, calling to one another, joking, past the racks of deer meat hung out to dry, older children chivvying the small ones away from campfires, horses in the long pasture. Not everyone left their womenfolk and children behind as we did. I wish they had: what if the elders choose to fight? What will happen to them all?

Led by the cool smell of fast-running water and the shouts of children filling buckets for their mothers, I make for the river: a wide sweep of water shaded by trees, hemmed by shores of flat grey pebbles. Sure enough, here's a gang of brats dipping pails, splashing each other and swimming. I pass them by, leaving their whooping and laughter echoing behind.

Who is he? What does he want?

If that boy is hunting me, I must think like the hunted: I'm going in. The water will break my scent. Leaving my boots and trousers on the bank, wearing only my thin tunic, I swim up to the river's bend where the pebbles and the tangled fronds of weed fall away further and further beneath me. I pull the leather ties from the ends of my plaits and tie them about my wrists, shaking out my hair. It's good to get it wet, to feel the cold of the river against my skin. I swim on my back, gazing up at the cloud-stained sky, the whiteness of the mountains.

He has followed me all the way from Samarkand. What does it mean? It is like spotting a glittering coin on the riverbed, grasping for it, but not being able to see clearly enough through the rushing water. When I am old and dying, and I look back remembering this boy, who will I see?

I break the water's skin. The heat of the sun is a shock, warming my head, my bare arms and shoulders. The quiet here rattles my peace. I hear the river's song, wind whispering through the trees, the harsh cry of a bird hidden among the darkness of the woods that crowd the riverbank, beyond the sweep of flat grey pebbles.

In my mind, I hear Mama's words again: *In those days, the Tribes used to trade far to the west, out of reach of the T'ang.*

And now I do see clearly; now I grasp the coin. I stand in the water, up to my waist, slippery pebbles smooth and hard beneath my feet. What if the boy was not looking for me, but the Gathering itself? What if he was not tending me in my dream, but about to do me harm?

Is he no saviour after all, but my enemy?

What if he is T'ang? He can't be. He has a spirit-horse. But at the talk-fire they spoke of rumours that men with the blood of the Tribes fight in the Empress's army for gold. Is that the truth behind my shadow-boy?

I dreamed of death and bloodshed. *Will it truly happen?* I had asked Shaman Tulan. *Not a foretelling but a warning,* he told me. A warning I failed to heed. *What have I done? How could I have been so foolish?* I was followed, trailed like a hunted hare. And I told nobody.

Now I hear it: the scream of a horse, a sound that stops the blood in my veins. I freeze. No one of the Tribes would goad our brethren into such fear or rage. The scream of a horse means one thing only: wall-dwellers are near. There are no settlements near here, no trader-inns. We are deep in the mountains of the Tribes and there are wall-dwellers here among us.

The scream came from the west. I cross the river, heading away from our camp, half wading, half swimming, shivering. Perhaps these wall-dwellers are just traders strayed from the Roads. I run up the bank, taking care not to shift the stones beneath my feet, into the forest, weaving between the trees, pine needles pricking my bare feet. The noise of our camp fades: my hearing is sharper than a dog's but even I hardly hear the hum and bustle of the Gathering: children laughing, crackling fires, women chatting.

But now I can hear something else, too: men talking,

many of them. Very many. I smell smoke, sharp sweat and fire-charred meat. Closer and closer I creep, through the trees. It's getting dark. Night draws near. The moon has risen above Claw Rock: I see it, a pale curve of light like a sliver of fingernail.

I stop and stare, shuddering in my wet shift.

The forest is riddled with men like fly-worms in old meat.

Clinging to the trunk of a pine tree, I watch them, heart pounding. Who are they? More Horse Tribers, come to join the Gathering? In the gloom, I catch sight of moonlight glinting off polished metal: swords, knives. Fighting men, soldiers: T'ang.

I could have told Baba that I had been followed, but I did not. I am shaman: I was born to protect our people. Instead, I lost my wits daydreaming about a green-eyed boy.

I led our enemy straight to the camp, like a sheep leading a wolf to the rest of the herd. This is my fault. My wolf-guide warned me.

I turn and run. I must find Baba. The time for secrets is gone.

10

Asena

"Baba!" *Oh, thank Mother Earth.* I see him, walking with Taspar on the way back from the talk-fire. Taspar looks unsteady on his feet: he's drunk.

"Asena!" Baba speaks sharply. "Where have you been all afternoon? Why did you run from the talk-fire? Shemi was left with all the tasks. And what did you mean by—"

"Baba, Uncle, you must listen. There are T'ang soldiers in the forest; I saw them—" *When this is over I will have to confess my part in this. My people will turn their faces from me for ever, even Mama and Baba, and I shall be alone.* Tears slide down my face.

"What are you talking of, girl?" Taspar demands, swaying. His breath stinks of kumis.

How are we to get away if half the men at this Gathering are drunk?

"Keep your tongue behind your teeth for once, brother,"

Baba replies, gripping my hand tight. "My own love, how many? Don't cry. All will be well – we must just move quickly."

I look from him to my uncle. Taspar shrugs his shoulders, and shakes away the fog of kumis. Now he's listening. Baba has never spoken sharply to him before, or not in my hearing at least. I can hardly bear to tell them.

"Enough to kill us all." My voice comes out in a whisper. "Very many. We must get away – everyone."

Baba grabs my arm, looking from me to his brother. Taspar nods. "Go," Baba says. "Tell whoever you can find. Kul and the others are still by the fire. Tell them to get the mothers and their bairns mounted up first. Find Shadow as soon as you can: you will be much safer on horseback. Taspar and I will round up as many folk as we can."

Taspar is already striding away, shaking off the last clinging tendrils of kumis-fog.

"Baba—" I don't want him to go; I don't want to leave his side. But he is right. We must split up: three folk alone can spread word quicker than three together.

Baba smiles at me, laying a hand on my shoulder. "Make sure you get to safety, with the horses if you can. Wait till we tell your mother about it – think of the look on her face."

I force myself to smile. Baba winks at me, turns and is gone, loping off into the shadows.

I burst into the first tent I come to. An old woman and three younger girls sit within, boiling mutton dumplings in a pot on the hearth. They stare at me as if I'm running mad.

One of the girls has a birthmark on her forehead, a deep red smear, a fingerprint left by the spirits when she came into the world.

"There's danger, men in the woods," I say. They stare. "Quick! Gather your things and go for your horses. If we scatter into the hills, there's still a chance."

One of the girls sniggers and I could slap her, but the old woman's nodding, her eyes lingering on my face. I feel sure I have seen her somewhere before. She lets a dumpling fall off her spoon back into the steaming pot and gets to her feet.

"I thank you, girl." She turns to her daughters or whoever they are. "What do you wait for – gather the food, and you, Gisha, run for your father. Rafi, where are your wits? Go for the horse-kind and tell whoever you meet on the way to do the same." She nods at me, standing up, wiping her hands briskly against her tunic. "You've done well this night, girl – now don't just stand there like a stone. Go!"

And now I know where I have seen this kindly, sharp-witted old woman: I saw her face night after night in my dream. She is the dead woman in my nightmare, blood trickling from her mouth, grey hair tangled over her forehead.

I run.

I lose count of how many folk I rouse, how many people I shake from their sleep, how many men I scream at on their way back from the talk-fire. Now there are people every-where I turn, moving quick, quiet in the shadows: women hauling laden packs, hushing sleep-slow children, men striding about with bows, leading horses. I am looking for

Baba. People pass me going the other way: everyone's surging to flee the camp. It's a race and they know it.

What was that sound: a dull, earthy thud? *Here it is again. And again.* I wheel around to look, and another arrow smacks into the ground and sticks there, quivering. Arrows? They are here already: the T'ang have attacked. Someone cries out. I hear a scream. Arrows fall around me, deadly rain – strange how you can't see them till they're whistling past your face.

Everywhere I turn, there are women running, small children in their arms, older ones racing to keep up. Some cry and scream, others are silent. And I see men, too, men with no spirit-horses: the T'ang. A young woman lies facedown, the dark shaft of an arrow sticking out of her back, a dropped cook-pot by her side. The air's thick with arrows now: like a flock of birds they deepen the sky's darkness.

It is happening. I am living my own nightmare. I could have stopped this.

I smell smoke now: I see it, curling grey against the night. Here's a tent in flames, its skins blackening and bulging, smoke pouring out. The air's full of shouting, screaming – a man in strange clothes runs towards me but I can't understand the words he speaks, and he has no spirit-horse. He is T'ang. I see a knife fly through the air. The knife hits him in the arm and I realize it was me who threw it. Mama will have sharp words for me when she finds out I've lost my knife. *Oh, Ma— Shemi, Shemi, where are you? Baba? Taspar?* I cannot find them. I call my father's name over and over again, but there's no sign of him. Here's the talk-fire, the smoking, trampled remains. Everywhere I look there are people lying broken on the ground. Children, too: I see a boy of no more than five summers with an arrow in his back.

How will I ever find Shadow? The T'ang attacked before we even had time to mount up; the herd must have fled. The Tribes cannot fight to win without our horse-folk. It's my fault: mine. I see our tents at last: one is burning, smoke billowing out.

"Baba!" I scream. "Shemi!"

But I am too late. Kul, Uncle Taspar and Shemi are here, after all. The din of battle seems to fade and all I hear is the beating of my heart. They lie on their backs just a few paces from our fire like dolls cast down by children. Killed by arrows, running towards a fight. Their spirit-horses have already fled. I step closer, first kneeling by Shemi, then Kul and Taspar, holding my hand against their throats. No rush of blood, no pulse of life. Why am I doing this? I know they are dead. Kul and Taspar are still holding spears. Useless against men with bows. Shemi's hands are empty. He ran to fight the T'ang armed with nothing but courage. It was not enough. I must give them the rites—

Red-hot pain bursts across my shoulder; I'm flung to the ground, face-down. I've been hit. I can't breathe: the air feels hot. Dark folds around me like a great swathe of black silk. All I can hear are men's voices, but so far away. Is that my father calling, *Asena, Asena, Asena!*

Baba—

11

Swiftarrow

He had done it at last.

He was alone with the girl in the clearing; the general and his soldiers still swarmed through the smouldering remains of the Horse Tribe camp, killing whoever they found alive. The girl lay as if dead, sprawling on her side so that the deep wound in her shoulder should not touch the ground.

He had done his duty at last: by the time two moons had grown large and died again in the night sky, he would cross the bridge into the Forbidden Garden with a new recruit for Autumn Moon. What did it matter to him if all the girl's kin were dead? Why should he care? But what about that man, crawling towards her with a wounded leg he couldn't stand on? Swiftarrow drew in a deep breath, trying to forget the anguish in the man's eyes, and his bloodstained face.

Don't take her! he'd called as Swiftarrow knelt, picking up the senseless, bleeding girl. *Asena, Asena, Asena! Don't take her, I beg you, don't take her—*

He was her father.

But then there was White Swan, helpless in the House of Golden Butterflies, at the Empress's mercy. *If I do not return, she will die.*

He turned away.

Walking through the shattered, burning camp with the girl in his arms, Swiftarrow had met a gang of Li's soldiers, grim-faced, swords out, beaten metal catching the thin light of dawn.

"What are you about, *Shaolin*?" the nearest of the soldiers had asked. "No prisoners: Li's orders."

"You do your tasks, I'll do mine," Swiftarrow had replied. "Don't bother yourselves going that way – there are none left alive."

At least he'd saved the life of her father.

He looked down at the girl. The skin of her neck pulsed with the swift, steady fluttering of life. Knotted, dusty black hair tangled over her shoulders, clotted with blood from the wound.

She should be dead, too.

He had pulled out the arrow from her shoulder, breaking the shaft first, silently thanking Autumn Moon for the silver phial of sleeping-draught and the healing herbs. He had cleaned the wound, salved it. It was bleeding less now.

The girl was strong. When he'd found her, he'd thought she was dead.

Through the camp he had carried her, a great heavy weight by the time he found his horse. *She ought to be grateful.* He wrapped his arms around his knees, gazing out at General Li's abandoned camp, the guttering fires, late-afternoon sunlight shafting down through the trees, flame-blackened deer bones left scattered across the pine needles.

I should not have done it.

Swiftarrow felt as if the ground were moving beneath his feet: he frowned, clawing back his hair. He'd had no choice: White Swan's safety depended on a barbarian recruit for the Forbidden Garden. What was it about this girl that shattered his peace? What was wrong with him? *Do your duty, get home and forget all this,* he told himself, furiously. He let out a long breath and looked down. Her hand had moved: a moment ago the fingers of her right hand had been lightly curled, as if she were holding something small and weak, like a baby bird. Now her fingers were spread out. His heartbeat seemed to grow louder, banging like a drum on New Year's Day. Her face was turned away from him; he could only see the back of her head, the dusty tangle of black hair. Had she woken?

Swiftarrow opened his mouth to speak and found that he could not. *What would I say, anyhow?*

She let out a small gasp, and Swiftarrow held his breath, afraid for the first time in years.

"Baba," whispered the girl, half sobbing. "Shadow. *Ah.*"

Swiftarrow wanted to tell her to be still lest she broke open the wound in her shoulder, but the words stuck in his throat.

I have destroyed her life. She turned her head to look at him, letting out a moan, her blood-smeared face tight with pain.

Her eyes opened wider when she saw his face. He reeled at the raw hatred. How was he going to get her back to Chang'an? It would be like trying to pick up a spitting, furious cat.

"You." The word seeped out of her mouth with a hiss.

Crying out in pain, she reached out and snatched the knife from his belt, dragging it from the leather sheath.

"No you don't." Moving fast, he reached out and grabbed her wrist.

"Let me do it." The girl was stronger than he'd thought, but she was not trying to drive the blade at his throat – she was trying to cut her own. Swiftarrow wrenched the knife from her grasp and she turned away, sobbing. He reached for the silver phial and let a few drops fall into her mouth. Very quickly, she fell quiet, lying limp on the forest floor like one of little Eighth Daughter's rag-cloth dolls. Silently, he thanked Autumn Moon for the potency of her sleeping-draught.

Swiftarrow leaned back against the tree trunk, sweat pouring down his face, eyes closed. He would have to keep her drugged all the way back. Two moons. Forty-two days. He prayed Autumn Moon had given him enough herbs.

"Found a pretty hostage, did you, holy boy?" It was Li, sprawling in a litter carried by two young T'ang soldiers still hollow-eyed with the shock of their first battle. They were just the sons of farmers. They ought to have been at home teasing the slave girls and helping their mothers brew lychee wine. One had blood on his face, the other stared firmly ahead, and Swiftarrow knew he was trying to forget the bleeding bodies, the crying children. He hid his surprise at the sight of them. So transfixed was Swiftarrow by his prisoner he'd not heard the men returning.

General Li smiled, his greasy face alight with triumph. "It seems the Shaolin are just as tempted by a lass as anyone else. I'm afraid you will still have to kill the girl, boy, when you are done with her – no prisoners. We have no need of hostages." Li raised his cup in a mocking salute and Swiftarrow wanted to break his fat fingers.

"She is not a hostage," he hissed, still leaning back against the tree, watching Li over the girl's slumped body. "She will be Shaolin. She is what I came to seek. Give me one of your women to tend her, O great General. The girl is a prisoner but she shall keep her honour, if I have my way."

General Li laughed, bidding the two young soldiers walk on with the litter. "Take as many of my whores as you wish. This day, I am inclined to be generous."

Swiftarrow watched him go and swore quietly. He could hear hoofbeats now, men calling to one another, dazed with the thrill of battle. He longed for the quiet of the Forbidden Garden, the rippling surface of waters overhung with willow, plum-blossom drifting on the breeze: peace. By the time he was there again, it would be summer, peaches growing fat on the trees, peonies breathing out their scent during the day, petals folding at nightfall.

He looked down at his prisoner. Her lean face was sunken and grey, her mouth slightly open. Swiftarrow felt as if he had shot down a swan – a swift graceful creature lying broken before him.

I have ruined her life.

12

Asena

My body is a prisoner, caught in the claws of sleep. My spirit-horse and I ride free through the blackness, trying to escape it, but just as I catch a hint of the light and colour of the world of men – the smell of wood-smoke, a snatch of talk in a language I don't understand – a bitter taste fills my mouth and the dark claims me once more.

Someone has drugged me with herbs, and I am too weak to stop them. I can hardly lift my hand. At least my shoulder hurts less now. *Ah, pull me under, darkness. Drown me. I cannot bear to live.* My wolf-guide is not here. Gone. I am drifting, lost in the spirit world without him. If I stray too close to the World Below, I will stay there, leaving my body behind for ever. Dead. I am so afraid.

I am inside myself once more. I've a sense of moving; I hear the wooden clatter of wagon wheels. Where am I going?

The bitter taste will come again soon, dragging me down into the shadows. The herbs they give me freeze my body and slow my mind so that I cannot make sense of anything. Even the food they force between my lips tastes of nothing but ash – how long will I be trapped? But I must swallow my panic, and I must use this time to think.

Why was I spared when so many died? Oh, Shemi, you are dead and it is my fault, my fault. Where are these people taking me? Questions flit about my head without end, like many fish in a pool. I do not even know how much time has passed since the night I lost Baba and Shadow, and the rest of my kin. Mama will be wondering what became of us. I dream of Mama and Aunt Zaka waiting night after night by the fire.

I didn't see Baba dead. To live, I must clutch at the hope he is still alive. When I wake, I will look for him till my last day on earth, if only to confess what I have done, if only to be turned away from my tribe for ever. Uncle Taspar is dead. Shemi. All of it my fault. How many folk at that Gathering lost their kin, even helpless little children? I am to blame. Tears seep from beneath my closed eyelids. They burn my skin. Oh, why can't I shake off this smothering sleep? Why don't my limbs obey me and move? I cannot even lift my little finger. The bitter taste touches my lips once more; sleep rises up to claim me and I ride my spirit-horse alone across the endless night.

I will escape my captors even if I die trying; and I will take revenge for each and every lost life.

Part 2

Chang'an: capital of the T'ang Empire

13

Swiftarrow
Two months later

Swiftarrow leaned back in the saddle, squinting against the late-morning sun. The westernmost city wall of Chang'an loomed ahead, crumbling mud ramparts held together by a thatch of weeds all baking in the sun. Silk flags mounted along the top flapped hard in the breeze, bright against the fierce, cloudless blue sky. They would have to wait while Li spoke with the guards. Swiftarrow was used to long, hot delays after all the checkpoints on the road east – clearly, the Palace had grown uneasy about the north-western border – but still he ached for the peace of the temple, for the whispering song of wind rushing through bamboo in the Forbidden Garden. Swiftarrow sighed.

In a few hours, I will be free of this hateful task.

Yet he knew it was not true. She would always be there to remind him of the life he had blighted. Perhaps Autumn

Moon would send the girl to learn the Shaolin Way in the Great Temple at the foot of Mount Shaoshi, many moons' ride east from the capital. But the Empress would surely want to keep her barbarian Shaolin, her new toy, in Chang'an.

Swiftarrow made for the wagon where his prisoner lay, weaving his mount amongst the desert-weary soldiers. The T'ang conscripts were now just as sun-browned and hard-eyed as General Li's Horse Tribers. *The Entertainment Ward will be drunk dry of rice wine this night and the concubines' mistresses will be rich by morning.* Swiftarrow frowned as he thought of his sister. *None of these fools can afford the attentions of White Swan. Not even General Li.* It was thin comfort.

Dismounting, saddle sore, Swiftarrow ignored the ache in his legs, patted the mare on her skinny flank and sprang up into the wagon, pushing aside the deer-hide covering.

"La, child – you do make me jump!" The concubine patted her moth-eaten hairpiece as Swiftarrow let the deer-hide fall into place behind him. Some of her real hair had escaped from beneath the lacquered coils, wispy and fine. She smiled, showing the remains of her teeth. "Poor lass – what's to be her fate, then? I've grown fond of the girl, tending her like a babe."

"Ask no questions, Mistress Orchid, and you shall be told no lies," Swiftarrow said. She shrank away from him, retreating to the far end of the wagon to gaze into her mirror. Swiftarrow looked down at his prisoner, kneeling before her. She lay so still, wreathed in drugged sleep, dressed in the ragged, travel-worn shift she'd been wearing when he'd found her with an arrow through her shoulder. Mistress Orchid had washed it, and now only a faint brown patch betrayed the bloodstains. Again, Swiftarrow saw the girl as she had been that day in Samarkand, running from him through twisting streets, full of bright, burning life. *And now look at what I've done to her.*

"You have done good work," he said to Mistress Orchid. "I will make sure you are well paid."

She turned from her looking-glass and smiled again. "Anything for a pretty face," she said. "And I don't mean hers – not that she is pretty, poor wench. It's what got me into this trade, I warn you. Did your mother never tell you to stay clear of ladies like me?"

Swiftarrow did not trust himself to reply. Leaning back on his heels, he watched the girl sleeping. She was much thinner, despite the broth Mistress Orchid had been spooning between her lips as she slept, and the morsels of boiled rice and dried pork Mistress Orchid had coaxed her to swallow while she was awake. The skin beneath her eyes looked bruised now: purple-grey, like the inside of a shell. The flesh had melted from her face; her cheekbones stood out like knife-blades. Her hair was combed and coiled about her shoulders; Swiftarrow felt a burst of sorrow for Mistress Orchid and her unlooked-for kindness. There was many a whore longing for a lost child. At the back of his mind clung shadowy memories of the House of Golden Butterflies. The other concubines used to look at him and White Swan with such great hunger in their eyes, pulling him up onto their laps, patting his head, combing White Swan's hair and pinning flowers to her skirt. He remembered the rose-oil scent of their heavy silk robes, their painted eyebrows and jangling bracelets.

Come, take my hand, White Swan used to say. *Let's hide in the dancing hall. They are bringing a leopard to show the men tonight. Maybe Cook will give us some meat to feed him.* Now she was one of them, a Golden Butterfly. Now she danced for the richest men in Chang'an. Swiftarrow drew his breath sharply; if he did not take care, the anger would burn him to nothing.

He would go to White Swan as soon as he could get away from the temple. *What will she say about this task of mine?* It was hard to know: his sister was good at keeping her true thoughts locked away, showing nothing to the world but her beautiful face. *It's all anyone cares for, anyhow. No one cares what she actually thinks, save me.*

Swiftarrow sighed and looked down at his prisoner again. Mistress Orchid was right: she was not beautiful, lying there so thin and still. A strand of black hair had slipped across her face. He reached out to move it, but stopped himself, pulling back his hand.

He whispered a curse. *Never again.* Never again would he carry out such a task, not even on the orders of the Empress herself.

14

Asena
Shaolin temple, Forbidden Garden

Last night, I awoke – to the rotting, foul reek of all wall-dwelling places. It was ever the same on the ride into Samarkand, but nothing can truly make you ready for the stench: the belly-churning body-waste of countless men, women and children, all flowing through the streets in a great river, the rotting food, unclean bodies, smoky cook-fires. I must be in a huge trading-place. But where? It isn't Samarkand, for that city always smells faintly of pepper-oil, and here I understand none of the talk I've heard in snatches. Is it Bukhara? Constantinople even? But there is a strange slant to the light, a different taste in the air. *Where am I?*

I've been left alone in a small chamber. There are wooden shutters drawn across the window but I can push them open to look out over a courtyard, a sloped rooftop and, beyond that, a mass of trees. The shutters still hold the faint, spicy scent of cedarwood. Whoever holds me captive does not fear that I might escape. I am weaker than a day-old kit, lying here on this pile of soft quilts. My hip bones are sticking out, my legs thin as sticks, fingers nothing but bone. I ache all over, and my hands shake. My right shoulder hurts, and when I reach to touch it, the skin feels different here – rougher. A scar.

And now I remember: I was wounded. Yet the wound has healed. A chill creeps down my back: when my uncle Taspar was shot in the leg three summers ago, the wound took nearly two moons to heal. Uncle Taspar. And I remember. My uncle is dead, the fault mine. Shemi is gone, and so have all the rest. Have I been captive for two whole moons? I have lost count of the days and nights, addled with herbs, helpless, unable to move. Whenever I close my eyes, I see my captor's looking back at me – glittering green, almond-shaped. I led him to the Gathering. I thought he was good, my saviour; I was wrong. A wave of sickening anger rolls through me. But I cannot only blame him. I must also bear the burden of guilt for those who died: men, women, children – every last one.

And all this time, I have been taken further away from Baba, if he is even still alive. Does he seek me along the Roads, asking in every trader-inn? I draw in a long breath. At the back of my mind are snatches of half-forgotten dreams:Mama hunched by the hearth, staring into the flames; Baba gazing into still water. We have been torn from each other but I will find them one day, I swear it now. I will kneel before them to offer my apology. It is worthless, but my duty all the same.

I may be too weak to climb, but I must get out of this place somehow. There is a heavy wooden door, but these wall-dwellers have some magic that keeps it fast shut. When I first woke, I crouched by it, pushing. No matter how hard I shoved, the door would not move. I shouted, but nobody came.

Yet I know there are people close by. I hear snatches of muffled talk, the clank of an earthenware pot being put down. This morning, when the chamber was filled with the grey light of dawn, the sound of chanting drifted from across the courtyard.

Why have I been brought to this place? Do I wait for my death?

I get to my feet and my whole body shrieks with pain. Leaning against the wall, I cross to the window, longing to feel fresh air against my face. Beneath my hand, the wooden wall feels faintly warm. Down in the courtyard, I see a little girl sweeping with a bundle of twigs tied to a crooked branch. She is the first person I have laid eyes on since I awoke. Like all wall-dwellers, she has no spirit-horse, and I shudder. Who is she? The child of my captors? Their slave? I stare, but the girl does not turn away from her task. She is clad in dusty black robes, her hair woven into a pair of plaits and cut bluntly above her eyes like a horse's forelock. Small clouds of yellow dirt curl up as she sweeps.

"Hie!" I shout, as if calling for Shadow across a long pasture. Tears prick my eyes because I will never see Shadow again, never trail my fingers through his white-gold mane. "Help me!" I cry. My voice is broken with misery: "Let me out!"

The little girl jumps and turns, looking up at my window with a round, pale face. She runs like a startled hare, leaving the bundle of twigs behind in the dust.

I gaze out at the empty courtyard again, breathless with loneliness. *Oh, where am I? What is this place?* If I crane my neck and lean out of the window, I can see a shining bronze bowl standing on a stone table. Beyond it, I catch a glimpse of a chamber with large doors opening out into the courtyard, but I cannot make out what lies within.

Oh, wolf, please come. If ever I needed a guide, it is now. But my wolf is gone, and the loneliness cuts at my heart like an iron knife. Why did he leave me? Was it the lie I told? Was it my secret longing for a boy? Boys are forbidden to me – and I knew it.

There is a low, soft creak as the door behind me swings open. I whirl around. A woman stands in the doorway beside a man with a scarred face. The little girl is hiding behind them. The scarred man and the woman are hairless, heads shaved bald as pebbles. They have no spirit-horses, either; their souls are shut tight within their bodies. Clad in the same dusty black robes as the girl, they both smile at me. How did they come so silently? I heard no footsteps, no talk, not even the soft hiss of three people breathing.

The man and the woman speak but I do not understand the words. Their voices are gentle, calm.

"Let me go!" I shout. "What do you want from me?"

They turn to the little girl huddling behind them. The scar-faced man takes her hand, which seems to give her the courage to step forward. The woman has an odd, hunted look about her, as if her mind is elsewhere, reliving something she would rather forget. Through my fear, I find myself wondering what is the matter with her.

"My name is Eighth Daughter," the little girl says, in strangely accented Horse Tribe. "This is Autumn Moon and Red Falcon. You have come to the temple of the Shaolin. The Empress wishes us to add barbarians to our number, and you were chosen. If you please her, you shall join us here." Suddenly the girl smiles. One of her front two teeth is missing. She cannot be more than seven years old. "And anyhow, I have always wanted another girl to play with, so I am glad."

I stare at her as the truth hits me: I have been taken to the Empire. I am a prisoner of the T'ang.

And what did she mean by, *If you please her?*

15

Asena
The Blind Trial, one ten-night later

I sit in the pool of warm water, watching steam rise up and
float out of the window. Mama spoke often of the bath-
houses in Constantinople, and told me many times they
were the only part of that city she missed. Now I know why.
Every knot of pain is soothed by the heat, and I ache each
day after stretching, lunging and balancing in the courtyard
with Eighth Daughter, following her every move. It is as if
we are learning the steps to a T'ang dance.

What is the meaning of this? I ask. *What are we doing?*

Autumn Moon says you must be strong, Eighth Daughter
always replies. *There is no use in following the Way with your
mind if your body is weak.*

I have tried telling her I don't understand, but Eighth
Daughter just shrugs and smiles. Although it is true that I
am no longer so weak; my body feels stronger and looser.

A tear slides down my face, down my neck, merging with

the bath water. I am so far from home. What is Baba doing now? Was he wounded? Is he safe? Each night I try again to fly to the World Above, seeking answers, but still I cannot shake free from my body. My wolf-guide is gone; the World Above is closed to me, as if a great rock has been rolled across a mountain path. Am I no longer a shaman at all? I am wracked by fear, pestering myself with unanswerable questions, but I cannot find calm.

The door swings open and Eighth Daughter comes into the bath-house with Autumn Moon, who is holding a pile of black cloth.

"Autumn Moon says you must come with her," Eighth Daughter tells me. She does not smile, this time. "You must come now."

Autumn Moon simply nods and shakes out her bundle: a black tunic and a pair of black trousers. She still wears that haunted, hunted look, as if her thoughts are half elsewhere. I wish she were not a wall-dweller, for then I could see her spirit-horse.

Once I am out of the water, dried and dressed, Autumn Moon bows low and speaks quietly.

"Autumn Moon says she is dearly sorry," Eighth Daughter tells me. "But she must bind your hands and your eyes."

"No!" I cry, but I have no time even to panic before my hands are tied together: Autumn Moon moves faster than a striking snake. A strip of black silk covers my eyes, and I feel her tying it firmly at the back of my head, taking care not to tug at my hair. I am sightless.

Autumn Moon has taken me outside. We have been walking a while now. It's a cool day: I feel mist beading on my skin, rough ground underfoot. Ah, but it's good to feel the earth under my feet again. No matter what happens, I stand on the broad back of Mother Earth, and Great Father Sky looks down on me once more. *See me, protect me.* I hear running water, birdsong. I smell the soft richness of flowers, too – strange. How can that be? The time for flowers is long gone: the steppe will be summer-dry by now, a vast plain of swaying, gold-dipped grass, the flowers all gone till next spring. But I am in the Empire, and perhaps the T'ang have magic to make plants grow when they should not.

We cross the water – it gurgles and rushes right beneath us – and I'm walking on something hewn of wood, worn smooth by countless feet. Still I catch that wall-dwelling stink – not so strong but lingering all the same: woodsmoke, dung, piss, strange spices, charring meat.

Autumn Moon quickens her step. We're growing near another wall-dwelling, another set of doors. I smell the press of folks' bodies, their breath, their oiled, scented skin, their sour sweat. How sickening these wall-dwellers are, huddling together in such a way; they are not like my kind, fresh and free, living under the sky beneath deerskin and larch-poles. Odd: now I'm blinded, my hearing's grown sharper still, I'm sure of it. I hear the soft rushing sound of many people breathing, the drumming of their hearts. How many? More than I can count on two hands. Some of them breathe quick and shallow, their hearts beating fast: they are afraid, or all a-thrill. What do they wait for?

I may be blind but every shred of my body is ready to move at the drop of a stone, even though my hands are bound.

We draw closer to the stink of gathered wall-dwellers. I hear a creak; a breeze rushes past my face as unseen guards open unseen doors.

Countless eyes are watching me: it's like a prickling rush of heat washing over my skin. My hands are released from the silk binding. I'm free, standing alone. I move to tear the blindfold from my eyes.

"There will be knives. There will be arrows. If you take off the blindfold, you will die." It is him. My captor. I would know that voice anywhere; it haunts my every dream. He speaks to me in a soft, low whisper. Furious hot hatred seethes in my belly. "Keep your eyes covered and she may let you live. Now listen." He steps away, and so does Autumn Moon; I no longer feel the heat of her body close to me.

Listen to what? I long to rip off the blindfold but I dare not. What fate has Autumn Moon delivered me to? She seems so gentle, so kind. But she is haunted: her eyes are always shadowed by a wrong she cannot forget—

The chamber rings with quiet. Still all I hear are folks' heartbeats, the slight squeak as someone shifts in his place on a stool, the soft rustle of silken cloth, birds calling to one another outside, the water's song.

"開始." It is a woman who speaks. Her voice is low,

smooth. I don't understand the words but I hear the thrill in her tone, mixed with scorn. From the sound of it, she sits at the far end of this chamber, right in front of me—

Wait? What's that?

It's the creak of drawn bowstrings. I'd know it anywhere.

They are going to fire at me—

The air hisses with arrows: one stirs up the air a finger's width from my left cheek. I drop to the ground, crouching like a cat ready to leap. The quiet's gone: I hear cheering, jeering, clapping, arrowheads landing with soft thuds on carpeted floor. What to do? I'm free to go anywhere; I am not bound – it's only that I can see nothing.

I swear everything's quieter to my left. Fewer arrows? But if I move, will they aim right at me? What manner of game is this, anyhow? No choice but to try: I can't stay here with arrows whistling past. I clear my mind; I think of nothing. I can't see you now; perhaps you can't see me, either, who- ever you are. I am not here. Don't look this way. I run, still half-crouched and flatten myself against a wall. Cheering – they're cheering, calling out.

The unknown woman calls out another command. I hear no more whistling arrows, no more bowstrings twanging. *What am I going to do? What deadly game is this?*

Think of nothing: be not here.

I reach out and feel something like a smooth tree trunk stretching up beside me. Is it to hold up the roof, like a tent- pole? I can climb a tree: I can climb this, surely. I run my hands up and down the slippery wood: it'll be hard, and

I have not half my old strength, despite the care of Eighth Daughter. But what choice is there?

Silk-blinded, alive with fear, I leap, catching the pole. Bracing myself against the wall, I scramble upwards, upwards. I am with Shemi once more, climbing the mulberries at the lake's edge, moving so clumsily he would laugh if he were really with me. Tears soak the blindfold. I will never climb trees with Shemi again. My right shoulder is a knot of pain. Still no arrows.

You can't see me: I'm not here.

I don't care what anyone says, I'm taking off this blindfold. But I daren't, not yet; what if someone catches a glimpse of fluttering black cloth? Higher, higher. The breath rasps in my chest. Surely they can all hear my heartbeat? It sounds like rolling thunder. *I must get away from this place: these people are crazed—*

What's that? I hear a high, singing note – cold iron slicing through the air. A dull thud in the wall just a hand span away from my face. I reach out and grasp metal. Knives. They are throwing iron knives. *What's this?* My head's struck something hard above. *The roof? No.* It's another of these thick wooden poles, like the one I'm climbing, but this one stretches out across open space. Reaching upwards with one hand, then another, I take hold of it. For a moment I'm hanging here like a bat in a cave. The air shifts near my face, and again I hear the bright hum of a flying knife: it stirs up a breeze as it passes my cheek. One of the T'ang can see me.

Think of nothing; think of nothing. It is just the same as travelling to the World Above with Shaman Tulan. It is just the same as hiding. You have done this many times.

I swing my legs up and grapple with the beam, clinging on with both knees. Now I'm hanging underneath like a dead deer carried out of the forest on a larch-pole. *Mother Earth, this hurts.* I've grown so weak; it's only the force of my rage and grief that keeps me moving. Who do these people think they are? I feel the weight of my damp braids dangling, pulling slightly at my scalp. There's shouting now, and the long hiss of another knife as it slices through the air, a finger's width away from my arm. *They can see me; they can see me.* I swing myself up so I'm sitting on the beam. Enough of this blindness; I don't care what happens. I snatch at the silk band, tugging hard – it won't come; I pull harder, digging my fingers into the knot at the back—

I'm hit – a lightning flash of pain behind my left ear. There's a clatter as the knife strikes the wooden floor below, missing a rug. The band comes away from my eyes, flutters to the ground like a dead black butterfly; the first thing I see is dark blood in the palm of my hand, my blood.

Sitting up, I look down on the chamber below and glimpse men and women dressed in bright silk robes. A handful of black-clad folk with their faces masked by black silk prowl among them like cats, knives in their hands—

The Shaolin: my captors are trying to kill me.

One hurls a knife – I can't tell who it is. The blade flies from their fingers faster than an eagle dropping out of the sky, blood-thirsting for her prey. I duck, flattening myself forwards against the wooden beam, which I now see stretches across the room to the far wall. It must be to hold up the roof—

I'm not here. You can't see me.

The place comes alive with another rush of hushed talk. One woman sits apart from the rest.

I feel the heat of Shaolin eyes. They see me when no one else can, but they've not spotted me yet. It is a battle of minds. I won't let them catch sight of me, my kind captors so ready to kill.

Sweat pours down my face. Blood runs warm down my neck. I feel the pain no more.

I have no weapon: I am helpless—

I've been seen. One of the Shaolin throws a knife, again, faster than an eagle-strike. Everything seems to slow down. Heartbeat hammers, knife flies through the air so graceful, like a deadly bird, thick quiet everywhere, all eyes on me.

I am Asena of the Horse Tribes: I shall not be defeated.

I reach out and pluck the knife from the air.

I catch it by the blade; my skin breaks, hot blood drips down my arm. There's a gasp from the gathering below. The woman who sits apart is smiling.

Like this, do you, Snake-heart? Is it good sport?

Flipping the knife and gripping the handle, I rise to a crouch, balancing on the beam. The last thing I need now is to come tumbling down to the floor: they'll butcher me. Knife clutched in one hand, steadying myself with the other, I run half-crouching along the beam. There's a window in the far wall, shutters wide open: my path to freedom. I see trees outside, the sky. If I die, it will be beneath the sky, not in this walled-up hole. I land in a crouch amidst the bright-silk folk who squeal and gasp. They fall back like petals tumbling from a dying flower.

Now the dark ones are all around me, the Shaolin, my captor, too, for I can see his spirit-horse, just a glimmer of a tossing mane. He is one of them.

The way out is but a leap away. I hold up the knife, ready to strike. As one, the Shaolin step closer. None holds a weapon. *Think you shan't need one? You are wrong.*

My captor speaks: "You were chosen. You have passed the test: you dodged blades and arrows sightless, with your hearing and your wits alone. Greet your Empress."

I hurl the knife to one side and leap towards him: I shall kill him with my own hands. I crash into him with the speed of a galloping horse. We fall to the ground as one, my fingers seeking his throat. He shall die for this. I will kill him. Voices rise all around us. He is stronger than me. He pins me to the floor, green-shadowed eyes fixed on mine. Again his touch burns me, as if we have both been set alight.

"Killer," I hiss, and again I snatch away the silken scarf covering his face. *"Killer."*

His beauty still knocks the breath from my lungs, even now. Even here. Hair touched golden by the sun, high arching eyebrows blacker than scorched wood.

I cannot move but I scarcely feel his touch; I know he is trying not to hurt me. He gets to his feet, drawing me upright. I stand facing him; he grips my arms and I cannot move. I am so tired that I begin to shake from my fingertips down to my feet.

"I am sorry," he whispers. "Forgive me."

"Murderer." I spit out the word and he looks away yet does not let go of me. I grip his wrists where he holds my arms. We stand so close, like a pair of lovers. We are the same, because I am as good as a murderer, too. I let him do it. I led him to the Gathering. And one day, I will kill him. I will put out the light in his pretty green eyes.

Somewhere, I hear a woman laughing.

Yes, and when I've killed this pretty boy, I'll take your life, too, Empress.

"I am sorry," he whispers again. His hand rests against my neck, just below my ear, as if he were about to kiss me. Why do I think so? Our eyes are locked together. I want the hatred in mine to burn him. His touch scorches me and I see nothing; I feel nothing. I tumble into darkness.

16

Asena
Temple of the Forbidden Garden, just before
dawn, several days later

Days and nights have passed, flickering like shadows. I have been watching the Shaolin, waiting for my chance to escape. Now I am going to take it.

Day has come once more. Their smiling god sits cross-legged against the far wall of this hall, wrought of shining metal. His sightless eyes stare peacefully at the shadows. Eighth Daughter calls him the Enlightened One. Flowers float in bowls of water at his feet. He is the chief god of the T'ang, but he cannot be a very powerful spirit. Not even the greatest shaman of the Tribes could trap our Sky Father in bronze like that.

These stone slabs are hard to sit on, but all the same, every day at the coming of first light all of us sit here doing nothing at all, save Hano the fat cook. *We are emptying our minds,* Eighth Daughter tells me, *so we can travel along the Way – the Middle Path – and leave suffering behind.*

It is the same this morning. Here they all are: Autumn Moon, Red Falcon, Eighth Daughter and Swiftarrow, too. The name suits him: he is fast, and a killer. He sits about twenty paces in front of me, cross-legged like the others. His hands rest on his knees. I stare at his back; I long for my loathing to scald his golden skin.

On the first day after the Blind Trial, Eighth Daughter spoke to me on Autumn Moon's behalf: "We are gravely sorry for your suffering, but in our hearts we are all glad you triumphed at the Trial. You are quite safe now, and no one here shall harm you. You were chosen to be Shaolin because you move like a shadow, but you will never be true Shaolin unless you leave behind hatred and fear."

"Tell your mistress I wouldn't hate anyone had my kinsmen not been murdered, my father lost."

Autumn Moon shook her head, smiling sadly, and the girl spoke for her again: "The truth of it is we create our own suffering, or at the very least we worsen it. We cannot choose what befalls us, but we can choose to face life with calm and bravery, rather than misery and terror."

I have never heard such drivel. Of course I cannot trust the Shaolin. How can they expect me to believe that I am safe here after the Blind Trial?

I am going to get out of this temple, out of Chang'an. There must be a merchant going west who will take me with him – I can mend broken bones, brew healing herbs to pay my way. And if I ask at every trader-inn, perhaps I will hear news of Baba. If he is still alive, I will find him; I swear it.

If he survived the ambush, he will be looking for me.

As I watch, the Shaolin sit while the morning dies around them. It is so quiet I can hear them all breathing slowly. The smell of boiling soup and wood-smoke drifts from the far side of the courtyard, along with the dank scent of standing water from the well. When the wind changes, I smell the city, too – dung, more smoke, rotting plums. A bird sings; it must be sitting in one of the mulberry trees clustering at the far end of the courtyard.

From across the courtyard, I hear the clatter of a wooden spoon dropped on the floor, followed by the thud of a heavy knife slicing through the roots and leaves these people eat. So the fat cook is busy.

What if I just get up and walk away? I rise. I'm on my feet. Not one of the Shaolin stirs. Slowly, slowly, I cross to the door, left just ajar. The smell of frying onions drifts inside. Oh, what I would not give for some meat: the Shaolin eat nothing but food fit for sheep, and not at all after midday. I am hollow. My bare feet make no sound on the floor. The old, worn stone is cold against my skin. I turn, looking back at the hall. All four Shaolin sit still, like rocks fallen out of the sky, clothed in black silk. Again, hatred seethes in my belly as my gaze falls on Swiftarrow. His head is slightly bowed; his hair has fallen over his face.

Killer. I cannot look at him.

If I do not try this now, I never shall. I run to the door and stop here, waiting. Nothing. They did not hear; they did not see. I look back into the hall. No one has moved. Now is my chance. I am going. I am leaving this place. I run across the courtyard. The inner gate is open; beyond it, I find myself in a forest of tall, green trees that look more like monstrous grass. Eighth Daughter says there is no word for this tree-grass in the tongue of the Tribes. In T'ang, it is called bamboo, she says.

I stop, listening hard. I hear the calling of a bird, wind rustling through the bamboo, the cook's knife chopping a steady beat. The first thing I will do once I have left Chang'an is find some real food: fire-hot meat and cool yogurt, salty tea.

Softly, softly, I close the gate behind me. It squeaks like a mouse. *A thousand curses!* I wait, cold with fear. Surely they heard? Surely someone will come? But no. Chop, chop, chop. The cook is still slicing sheep's food for the pot; he does not even pause.

I must take my chance. *Which way is the city?* Closing my eyes, I listen. I hear the far-off hum of many voices, an ass braying, chickens squealing, the bark of a dog – all half veiled by the endless song of wind rushing through bamboo. I run towards the clamour of Chang'an, south-west through the green forest.

The bamboo is behind me now; I run across a bridge over a pool fringed with willow trees. Fat lily-flowers float on the water's skin, which is dappled with bubbles where fish like shards of gold snatch flies. Is that laughter I hear, just faintly, borne behind me on the wind? I have no time to stop; I must run. The sounds of the city grow louder with every step; I am getting near. I hear a rush of voices, the squeak of wooden cartwheels; a child cries out. The smell of wood-smoke and dung has grown stronger, tickling the back of my throat. To the south, the sky is hazy with smoke. There it is again: laughter, yet the sound does not come from the city, but from behind me. *Am I followed?*

Think of nothing and you shall be as nothing.

I have no time to fear; through the trees I fly. The rich scent of bark and sap lights a flame of longing for home that burns my heart. Tears stream down my face as I run. *Mama, O Baba. Baba, I shall find you if I can just get away—*

Darken your mind and you shall not be seen.

The garden wall rises up before me – crumbling old mud bricks stitched with sun-baked weeds. Easy to climb. I fly at it, digging my fingers and bare toes into the cracks. It's a long drop down to the street, but I have no choice. Just below me, a man is selling fish from a basket; a dog noses through the dust. Gasping, I land a hand span away from the fish-seller – who does not see me. The dog looks up and howls. He backs away, showing his teeth.

I am not here; I am not here. I cannot help smiling at the thrill of it, even though my heart drums faster and faster with fear. The dog whines. *Well, never mind, my friend, I shall soon be gone.*

I dodge market stalls selling bales of cloth, heaps of gnarled roots and barrels of spices. A crowd has gathered around a boy beating a jackass that will not move; they're shouting, laughing. I can't understand what they are saying, but you can safely wager they're all yelling useless advice. It is always the same in trader-towns when there is a beast that will not be moved; wall-dwellers never think to ask the animal why he wishes to stay where he has been put— *Wait? What was that?* The back of my neck prickles. Is someone watching me? I glance over my shoulder but everyone is still looking at the boy with his flea-bitten jackass. A pair of young women walk by, giggling over some secret joke – their eyebrows have been shaven off and drawn in higher with greenish-blue paint, giving them an odd, surprised look. A little girl runs past with a bucket full of water, splashing my legs. None of them see me, yet I can't escape the sense that someone is watching. It is just like in Samarkand—

A hand rests on my shoulder. Cold fear drenches me from head to foot. I turn, looking up into the face of the fat cook from the temple. Hano. It is as if he has just stepped out of – nothingness. So he is true Shaolin, more than just a servant, after all. He smiles at my shock, shaking his head. I am caught. His grip is not heavy, but it is sure. He takes my hand, as if leading a child. I will not get away from him. He speaks to me gently in T'ang: I do not understand the words, but his voice is so kind I weep.

Baba. Mama. How will I ever see you again?

Tears stream down my face but I no longer care enough to hold them back. I understand now: the Shaolin will never let me go. I cannot escape them.

I am trapped.

17

Swiftarrow
In the palace, several days later

Swiftarrow knelt, bowing so low his forehead rested against the Persian rug. Ringing with voices, the chamber was heavy with the scent of perfumed courtiers and wet silk. A servant had drenched the silk in clean water and hung it from the window-shutters, but even so the warmth grew more oppressive with every moment. He was half fainting in the heat. *How much longer?* He listened to the dripping water, trying to ignore the ache in his legs from kneeling so long. He caught hold of snatches of talk, and let go again, breathing deep.

"My dear, you *must* have heard what Lady Jeng did to her poor maidservant" … "Four cartloads of purple silk, spilled all over the highway. Imagine—" … "She cut open the girl's eyebrows and filled the wounds with ochre. Well, it doesn't do to let one's maidservants look too pretty, does it?" … "He was caught in her chamber by the oldest son. Can you bear it?"

Keep to the Way, Swiftarrow told himself. *Don't stray.* They were nothing more than brightly feathered birds, these courtiers, these fluttering fools. They ignored him, stepping around him as if he were a wooden stool. He could smell the camphor they rubbed into their feet to hide the stink of summer sweat, the dried herbs their costly robes were packed in over winter to keep out the moths.

He thought of her. Asena.

She had tried to escape, of course. And of course she had failed, brought back to the Forbidden Garden by Hano, dusty and defeated. He had felt the depth of Asena's despair before they even came in through the courtyard gate. He had seen bottomless hate in her eyes when Hano led her in, telling her kindly to eat, for she had earned a good feed by running so fast. But Asena had eaten nothing, just knelt by the table, staring dead ahead, looking at no one as tears streamed down her face, not even blinking when first Autumn Moon had tried to comfort her and then Eighth Daughter.

She is good, Eighth Daughter had whispered to him later, once she had garnered the full tale from Hano. *She got all the way to the market before he caught her. Sister Autumn Moon had is pleased with you for finding such a talented girl.*

Swiftarrow suppressed a sigh. He was ready to be hated. He knew he deserved it. But now if they passed by one another in the courtyard or the hall, Asena looked away or stared straight beyond him. It was worse than being hated. He would have to get used to thinking of her as Asena, not just a nameless girl, a prisoner.

It was as if she did not even see him. And yet he wanted to take her hand. He wanted to feel the knot of fire that had scorched him when they first touched. That was the truth of it.

Don't be such a fool, he told himself. *She is just a ragged barbarian, and you've ruined her life. She detests the very ground you walk on.*

At last, someone clapped briskly, and quiet fell across the chamber. "Rise, my little half-breed." Drawing in a long breath, Swiftarrow sat back on his heels, still looking down.

He was here – Swiftarrow knew it: Lord Fang. He had picked out that soft, mocking voice from among the gossipy whispering. It would be foolish to look, and he had been kneeling long before the courtiers came in. Still looking down at the winding Persian flowers woven into the rug, Swiftarrow felt the heat of many people staring.

"La, see how he flushes," whispered one lady to her companion. "So delicious."

Oh, sweet ancestors, preserve me. Not this again.

"Take care, dear cousin," the Empress said. "Have you forgotten the Shaolin can hear more acutely than dogs? See, you have made the boy ashamed of his beauty. Child, look at me. Am I not lucky to have so fair a weapon?"

A rush of sighs fluttered about the room like tiny birds as Swiftarrow raised his head to look. Sitting cross-legged on a red couch of carved carnelian-stone, the Empress was dressed this morning as a man: she wore simple robes stitched so fine they appeared seamless, but her piled-up hair was dotted with small peonies and her shaven eyebrows drawn in with sea-green paint. Her forehead had been dusted with yellow good-fortune powder, very bright against her pale skin, like the light of the sun.

Mad as a basket of snakes, Swiftarrow thought, waiting for her to address him again. Speaking out of turn was a fool's trick; men had died for less. He pushed the thought from his mind. *Where was the Emperor? Too sick to leave his bed again? What a fine empire this is, ruled by a shaking, palsied wreck and his spider of a wife.*

The Empress smiled at Swiftarrow, showing blackened teeth, and it took all his self-mastery to crush a great shudder of disgust. "I am pleased with your work," she said. "Autumn Moon tells me the barbarian girl is greatly skilled and shall do well once she is fully trained. Did you remember to thank my dear General Li? Were it not for him, you would never have found her, after all."

Fat, lying hog – I should have known he would take the praise for that. But Swiftarrow wished it were true and he had not been the one to ruin Asena's life.

He nodded. "Yes, Your Imperial Majesty. When I next have the good fortune to cross paths with General Li, I will thank him. I could not presume to seek out his attention but must wait till he sees fit to notice me."

The Empress smiled again. "Good. Now, Lord Fang – what do you make of your Shaolin boy? Ought we to give him another task?"

"I scarcely know, Your Majesty." The voice was slow, languid, as if the speaker had only just woken.

Swiftarrow's heartbeat quickened and he glanced down. *I am worth no more than a half-forgotten painting, a new bolt of printed silk, a caged bird he admires when the fancy strikes.* There was no use in wishing that Lord Fang had any other use for him. He stared at the rug, woven flowers and strange beasts all twining about each other.

Light footfalls and the rustle of silk broke the quiet. Still Swiftarrow did not look up, even when he felt the cold touch of ivory at his throat; a long, pointed nail-guard grazed the skin just beneath his chin. "Look at me, child," said his father.

The scent of rice wine stung Swiftarrow's eyes. His first memory of Lord Fang was laced with the rich smell of peonies drifting around the House of Golden Butterflies and the sour reek of wine. He could still hear the echo of his mother's voice: *Kneel before your father, my dear one. He has made a special journey to see you.*

"I dare not gaze upon my most esteemed parent."

Laughter floated around the chamber. The nail-guard dug harder into Swiftarrow's throat and he looked up into the face of his father.

"Such impudence." Lord Fang let each word fall from his lips like a drop of cold water. Swiftarrow stared back at him, savouring the small victory. Lord Fang's hair was streaked with grey now, the lines around his mouth and eyes drawn deeper. In the House of Golden Butterflies, the concubines still whispered of him. *Lord Fang and your mother,* they said, *such a fair couple there never was before; and has not been since. They were surely blessed by the goddess of the moon. But, oh, they were doomed from the start.*

"What a very pretty boy you are," Lord Fang said, softly. "Dagger-tongued and foolish, too: just like your mother in every way." Another light burst of laughter rippled about the chamber.

Swiftarrow looked away. His eyes burned. *I hate him, I hate him.* Sharpened by regret, his hatred cut all the deeper. He wished he had enough regard for Lord Fang to speak with respect. But it was not so. A sole tear ran down his face and shame washed over him like scalding water.

Lord Fang smiled, lazily. Reaching out, he let the tear slide onto his fingertip, sighing, "Full of such fire, you are, boy. Ah! So very like her. I ought to write a poem about you. I wrote several about your mother. I have written none about your sister. I do not think it would be quite proper." He laughed, at last moving the ivory nail-guard away from Swiftarrow's throat. Swiftarrow did not move; he knew the disgrace of weeping would haunt his sleep for nights.

Lord Fang turned to the Empress, who was now reclining on the carnelian couch. She watched them; a smile pinched her painted lips.

"Your Imperial Highness," he said. "I shall be most honoured if you will allow my son to serve you again."

I am here to amuse you, Swiftarrow thought, *just as my mother was before me.*

The Empress laughed, stretching like a cat. "How wonderful." She sat up, looking around the room at her courtiers, who shrank away like chastened children. "What are you all doing, standing about like stuffed pig bladders? Tear your eyes from Lord Fang's lovely son; none of you shall have a taste of the boy."

There was a moment of shocked quiet, a suppressed giggle and then a rush of chatter as the courtiers turned back to their gossip.

Swiftarrow looked down at the rug again, sure that the weaving flowers and beasts would tangle about among his dreams.

"So, what would Your Highness have the boy do?" Lord Fang sounded bored.

"Is it not time the child knew his kin, Fang?"

Swiftarrow heard the smile in her voice and wished he could see the horror writ across Lord Fang's face, but he did not trust himself to look up. *My father would rather stick knives in his eyes than admit me to the bosom of his family.*

The Empress laughed. "Do not fear. I am not suggesting that you take home your whore-house leavings. Your poor wife! Does she not suffer enough with the summer fever? No, no. Look at me, boy."

Swiftarrow obeyed.

She smiled again. "No, Fang – the boy must go to his Horse Tribe brethren. I grant that the tribes Lord Ishbal sent did fine work for General Li, but I fear very much that Ishbal and his barbarians now plot against me – against my dear husband. Go to their dirty little camp outside the east wall, boy, and find out if it is so." She raised one hand to her mouth in mock horror. "How awful if all those horse-riding barbarians were to join forces from one end of the Roads to another! Only think of the smell."

Swiftarrow swallowed his horror, making sure his face remained a blank mask of obedience. *I should tell her I refuse. I cannot do it again.* In his mind, he saw the burnt and ruined Horse Tribe camp – the fleeing horses, broken bodies, the smouldering tents. He saw the agony in a father's eyes as his daughter was taken away.

The Empress's smile faded; Swiftarrow knew he must speak. Lord Fang was frowning at his silence. *I've angered him,* Swiftarrow realized with a jolt of satisfaction.

"Your Imperial Majesty, I shall do whatever you most desire." Swiftarrow bowed low again till his forehead touched the ground. He was a coward. He had promised to obey even though he knew it was wrong. He could not bear it. *I am not here.* A gasp rose up from the gathered courtiers and Swiftarrow heard the Empress laughing as he ran to the door, unseen by all. *Coward,* he cursed himself. *Filthy coward.*

Swiftarrow wished himself into nothing, but as he ran, he wondered what price Lord Fang would demand.

18

Asena
Shaolin temple, Forbidden Garden,
later the same day

I stand facing Autumn Moon in the temple hall.
We are alone, save little Eighth Daughter, who sits
cross-legged like the statue of the Enlightened One,
watching Autumn Moon and me. Streams of light the
colour of golden ale wash across the stone floor from the
high, latticed windows. Autumn Moon watches me, and
I watch her. Her bald head glints in the sunlight, her face
is narrow and lean and she has barely any chin: in truth,
Autumn Moon reminds me of the fish that swim in the
green, shadowy pools outside in the Forbidden Garden.
Yet there is another kind of beauty in her – when she
moves, it is like watching a bird in flight, but now she
is still, she is like a pillar of rock out in the wild steppe:
utterly motionless.

She bows her head and looks up. Autumn Moon rarely
smiles, but often I catch the light of kindness in her eyes,

behind that hidden sorrow. I wonder again what she has done, what haunts her so.

"Look," she says in T'ang – Eighth Daughter has taught me a handful of words – and lifts one hand, pointing at the Wall of Beasts. Every time I see this wall, the wonder of it makes me stare. How is it done? Birds in flight, huge, prowling cat-like creatures, bears, leaping wolves, all frozen for ever on silken strips that hang fluttering gently from the roof. They are not real birds and wolves, of course, I know that; they have been made by the scar-faced one, Red Falcon, who used to paint for the Emperor before he came to live among the Shaolin. But I had never seen anything like it till I came here. As the silk shifts in the breeze, the beasts seem to move of their own will, just like real creatures. There are black shapes painted here, too, in long rows. These mean nothing to me, but I think it is this magic the T'ang use to talk to one another without speaking: the same as speech, only silent.

Autumn Moon smiles at my wonder and moves closer to the rippling silk, pointing at a running wolf. Strange how she chooses the wolf. I point at my chest.

"Me," I say. I don't know the T'ang word for spirit.

Is it even true? My wolf-guide has left me. I am no wolf-girl any more.

Autumn Moon nods, slowly. Now she points at herself and says something I don't understand.

"Sister Autumn Moon says that, over many years, the Shaolin have learned how to move with the grace and speed of beasts and birds," Eighth Daughter explains. "Although there are many foolish tales of the Shaolin using these skills to defeat great armies of warriors, in reality we use them to fight our own selves – our anger, selfishness and greed – so that we can keep to the Eightfold Path and achieve eternal peace when we die. She says that your heart-sickness and your anger will be eased by learning how to do the same. So now she is going to show you the wolf." Eighth Daughter grins. "Don't be afraid, Asena. It's easy: I can do this and I am smaller than you."

"Wait. Tell me," I demand. "This seeking for peace is not your only aim, is it? Let us be honest with one another: you have not the courage to kill with your own hands, but hide and sneak like shadows, delivering innocent men and women to their deaths just because the Empress has chosen it."

Eighth Daughter frowns. "I – I don't know." She turns and speaks rapidly to Autumn Moon, who nods, answering in a quiet voice: this is what haunts her, the killing, the deaths she has caused.

"She says it is very hard, but that we have a duty to the Empress as well as to ourselves. And now she will show you the wolf."

Eighth Daughter falls silent. Autumn Moon is watching me so closely I feel as if she can see the colour of my thoughts. Taking a few steps away from me, she stands still, breathing deep: I see the rise and fall of her thin chest.

She runs at me with the speed of sky-fire flashing across the night and I duck, putting up my arms. Now I'm helpless on my back – she's got me pinned by the shoulders. Autumn Moon kneels on my legs, fixing them to the floor. The pain is bone-deep; she has me like a wolf with its prey. Shocked by the fall, I can scarcely breathe. Autumn Moon is smiling, and speaks a word I don't know. *What am I meant to do now?* I would kick, but I cannot move. *Oh, Mother Earth, it hurts.* I try to roll, but I cannot. I'm helpless. At last, Autumn Moon lets out a short burst of laughter and gets up, releasing me. I stagger to my feet, rubbing my thighs where her knees dug in. Eighth Daughter laughs, too, and claps her hands.

"You." I know this word. Autumn Moon is speaking to me. She takes a few paces backwards and stands still, arms loose by her sides, waiting. Again, I catch a glimpse of that shadow about her eyes.

I turn and look at the silken wolf rippling against the wall, stirred up by the breeze.

Autumn Moon watches, waiting. I must strike her the way she struck me, in the manner of Blue Wolf hunting Red Deer through the forest. I draw in a long breath, steadying myself: *I am back with my people, deep in the tangled green-wood at night, before I ever became shaman and was forbidden the hunt. We are close about the fire. Now we hear it: the long, drawn-out moaning cry of the wolf-kind. Wolves don't like fire, but if their hunger bites deep, they'll come for us. I let my spirit fly free of my body, rising higher and higher. Wolves weave through the trees – nothing but dark shapes from this height. My soul sinks down, down into the body of the largest wolf; now I am the wolf and the wolf is me. We are one. My soul is inside him.*

Together, the wolf and I leap.

I look down and I see Autumn Moon on the floor beneath me, breathless. My hands press down on her skinny shoulders, but only one of my knees is pinning her leg. With the other, she kicks so fast I've not time to even blink, and rolling sideways, she snatches herself away from my grip. Now I'm face-down on the hard floor, one arm twisted behind my back.

She barks out a short, dry laugh and lets me go, calling out to Eighth Daughter. I sit up, rubbing my arm, half-dazed.

"Autumn Moon is pleased with you," Eighth Daughter tells me. "She says you will soon know how to leap like a wildcat and fly like a swallow."

Autumn Moon grins. "Good," she says. "Good. We are the wolf. You know. Now this." And she points at the flying swallow. But just as she stands up, Autumn Moon and Eighth Daughter both turn their heads to the courtyard. Autumn Moon frowns.

"Someone's coming," Eighth Daughter says. "One of us, running very fast. I hear the beating of his heart." She means one of the Shaolin. My senses are sharp enough to have brought me through the Blind Trial, but will I ever be able to hear so keenly as the rest of the Shaolin?

Swiftarrow flies into the hall. His spirit-horse rears on her hindlegs, mane tossing: a much stronger creature than when I first saw him. *Murderer, filthy murderer.* He stumbles to a halt before us and I look away; Eighth Daughter stares open-mouthed at his lack of grace, and he unleashes a torrent of angry words at Autumn Moon. Autumn Moon watches calmly, saying nothing. He shouts at her again, the first time I have heard a raised voice in this temple. Eighth Daughter's cheeks are flushed deep red. Is she ashamed on Swiftarrow's behalf? For a moment I wish I knew what he was saying, but why should I care about him?

At last, Autumn Moon raises one hand, palm outwards, as if pushing away Swiftarrow's anger. He falls silent, standing so still the life seems drained from his body. Autumn Moon speaks to him as if no one else is here, and his spirit-horse lies on her side, fading again. Swiftarrow turns and walks out of the hall, back into the courtyard.

Autumn Moon does not watch him leave, just bows at me, speaking quietly to Eighth Daughter, who is still red in the face. She jumps up, pulling at the sleeve of my black silk tunic, so cool and still unfamiliar against my skin.

"Come, Asena!" Eighth Daughter grins at me. "Autumn Moon says it is time to eat. Hano has brewed a good broth for us."

The Shaolin may use their skills to fight anger and selfishness, but I intend to use these same tricks for another purpose. *You will save us from the T'ang,* Shaman Tulan told me. I have failed my people once, but that does not mean I will do so a second time. Swiftarrow was nothing but a tool in the Empress's hands. Killing him would be a waste of time. But if the Empress herself were to die, the T'ang would have bigger fish to trap than the Horse Tribes. The Emperor is weak. They say he is too sick to leave his bed. Without the

Empress, the Imperial throne will be as good as empty, the Tribes safe. I will have paid all I can give for those who died at the Gathering: my own life. I will not kill the Empress and survive.

I shall learn everything Autumn Moon has to teach me, and I will do it well. I will sneak into the Empress's chamber more silently than a cat, and I will leap at her throat like a wolf bringing down a deer.

19

Swiftarrow

Moon-silvered clouds hung above Chang'an, pale against the black sky. In the Forbidden Garden, the temple was quiet. In one chamber, a lamp and a brazier had been lit, casting a puddle of yellow light out of the window. Long shadows stretched across the courtyard. Red Falcon stepped out of the chamber, closing the door behind him, and crossed the courtyard into the hall.

From beyond the darkness and peace of the Way, Swiftarrow felt a hand on his shoulder. He returned to his senses with a jerk, aching all over. Night had fallen and the temple hall was dark. Silk drapes fluttered, pale and moonlit. Red Falcon's painted beasts were all in shadow now. Swiftarrow's throat ached with thirst. Not a drop to drink nor a mouthful of food had passed his lips since dawn, when he'd left for the palace. The air smelled of incense and freshly fallen rain. He sat back on his heels and turned to find Red Falcon kneeling at his side, scarred face twisted into a smile.

"Come. Autumn Moon has a wish to speak with you."

Swiftarrow sighed, longing for lost peace, trying to shut out the echoes of Lord Fang's mocking voice. Yet it was not only Swiftarrow's father who haunted him, but she – Asena. Even in the hall today she had stared past him as if he were not there, then simply looked away. Whenever he closed his eyes, he saw her face.

"Brother," he said, "it took me long hours to find peace. Am I now to be chastised?"

Red Falcon helped Swiftarrow to his feet. "Do not drag me into your battles. Hano heard you blow up like a handful of dragon-powder all the way from the cook-room. The poor man nearly sliced off one of his own fingers." He stopped smiling. "No, it's to my mind that she wishes to speak with you of some other matter."

"What, then?"

"Let Autumn Moon tell you herself." Red Falcon laughed. "Ah, but we have been trying to teach you patience for ten years. Come."

"You might at least try harder, then," Swiftarrow said, but Red Falcon only smiled, and together they crossed the courtyard, arms about each other's shoulders.

Swiftarrow followed Red Falcon into the painting chamber. The air was heavy with the musty smell of ink and damp silk. Autumn Moon sat alone near the brazier, holding out her hands to the warmth. A tray of cups lay before her beside a porcelain jug. Swiftarrow caught the scent of stewed flowers as he sat down: jasmine tea. He bowed, meeting his mistress's calm gaze.

"I bid you both goodnight." Red Falcon bowed and went out, shutting the door.

"Pour, Swiftarrow, I beg you."

"Forgive me, O temple-sister." Swiftarrow lifted the jug and poured a share into each cup. "I am sorry."

Autumn Moon's hand shook very slightly as she picked up her cup, and Swiftarrow stared in alarm. "You came rather too close to speaking publicly of your task for the Empress: you know it is forbidden to do so." She sighed. "Yet what concerns me more is your uncontrollable passion. Such anger never leads to good," she said. "But in truth it is I who must apologize to you, Swiftarrow. I was wrong to choose duty to the Palace over the Path of Peace: we should not be laying information before the Empress, knowing men die as a result." Autumn Moon shook her head. "Red Falcon, Snake-eye and I have all whispered secrets to the Empress that led to bloodletting. We as good as killed those men ourselves. But I should have refused when she asked for you, Swiftarrow. You have not yet fifteen summers—" She broke off, closing her eyes, steadying herself. "Have you spoken to Hano or Red Falcon about where Snake-eye has gone?"

Swiftarrow shook his head.

Autumn Moon took a sip of her tea. "While you were gone, I sent him to Mount Shaoshi."

He drew in a sharp breath. "All the way to the Great Temple?"

"Yes. It was necessary. I believe we should return there. Twenty winters ago, the Shaolin came to Chang'an with the Abbot's permission. I could not go back to Shaoshi without it. We cannot escape the Empress altogether, but if we get beyond her immediate reach, I hope she will turn her interest elsewhere once the anger has passed, as a child forgets a lost toy."

Swiftarrow stared at her a moment, turning over the news in his mind. If the Shaolin left Chang'an, he would not have to infiltrate Lord Ishbal's camp outside the city walls and betray the Horse Tribes again. And perhaps, in time, there would be a day when Asena did not look straight through him. He closed his eyes and saw her long dark eyes, the slope of her shoulder, the curve of her waist.

What am I thinking? He longed to hold the girl he had captured. *Thrice-cursed fool,* he told himself, furiously. *What good will this serve? It will lead to nothing but trouble.* But he could not escape it: he would have given anything for Asena not to hate him.

"Well?" said Autumn Moon, giving him a searching look. "Does the news not please you? Swiftarrow, since you came back from the west, you have been either snapping like a wounded dog or more dazed than a toad in a barrel of ale. What else troubles you, besides the Empress's demands?"

He said nothing, staring at the steam rising from his jasmine tea.

Autumn Moon sighed, taking a sip from her own cup. "Again, the fault is mine," she said. "When the Empress demanded you bring me a barbarian to train, I should have told you not to take a girl. Swiftarrow, I ask you to remember what is forbidden in the temple. Seven years shall pass before you must choose whether to take final vows but, even if you leave us, do not forget that heedless desire only causes pain. And Asena is alone, without her family and grieving for those she has lost as a result of our actions – consider her peace of mind."

"You need not worry! She despises me." He looked away. Why did Autumn Moon see so much? Could he hide nothing from her?

She sighed, shaking her head. "Poor girl. I am glad to have her among us, but the sooner we are all free of the Empress's whims, the better. Tread carefully, Swiftarrow. Do not be ruled by your heart."

"What about my sister?" Swiftarrow said, quickly. "Autumn Moon, I cannot leave her in the House of Golden Butterflies for ever. They talk of her beauty from tavern to palace but what kind of man would take her to wife?"

Autumn Moon took a sip of tea. "White Swan knows what we intend. Red Falcon went to the monastery in the Entertainment Ward last ten-night, when your sister was listening to the sutra in the meadow with the rest of her kind. If White Swan chooses to come with us, we will be honoured to escort her. But we shall go nowhere till Snake-eye safely returns with word from the Great Temple. The

Abbot shall choose our path. My dearest hope is that he will allow us to leave Chang'an."

"But what if the Empress hears of this before Snake-eye returns?" Swiftarrow pushed away the thought of Snake-eye caught travelling without Imperial permission, questioned. Tortured, even. It was unlikely that Snake-eye would be snared by the Empress's troops, and yet still possible.

Autumn Moon nodded, slowly. "Then let us hope that she does not hear of it."

In the same instant, Swiftarrow and Autumn Moon froze at the sound of distant hoofbeats.

She took another sip from her cup, unruffled. "An eager visitor, indeed."

"I shall wake Red Falcon and Hano."

Autumn Moon smiled. "You have your faults, Swiftarrow, as have we all, but sluggish wits is not usually one of them. Consider it: who would be foolish enough to attempt harm to the Shaolin in our own temple? And I hear only one horseman. No match for us."

He shrugged and followed her to the window. She pushed open the carved cedarwood shutter, and moonlight flooded into the chamber. The courtyard was silent, but Swiftarrow could hear the horseman coming closer and closer. The drumming hoofbeats grew muffled as the rider took his mount across the grass by the Pool to Release the Living, then sharper as they crossed the beaten-earth outer courtyard.

Swiftarrow's heart thudded; he drew a long breath,

calming himself. Autumn Moon stood steady as a mountain. The inner gate flew open and a horseman rode into the courtyard, the long sleeves of his robe billowing, hair flying free: Lord Fang.

"He is drunk." Swiftarrow felt a chill slide down the back of his neck. Not once in the last ten years had Lord Fang come to the Forbidden Garden.

"Never mind that," Autumn Moon said. "Come with me and we shall see what he wants."

"I do not care what he wants," Swiftarrow replied. It was a lie.

20

Asena

Eighth Daughter and I sit on her bed wearing only our night-tunics, linen coverlets tangled about our legs. By the moon's light, I am weaving her hair into fresh plaits, combing out the tangles, just as Mama used to do for me every night, and I for her.

We each draw in a sharp breath, rushing to the window as a rider on horseback thunders into the courtyard, the long sleeves of his court robe flying out behind like flags. The gelding's fear sickens me; I reach out for his mind, which is a-whirl with swirling clouds of crimson and black. *Be calm, brother. Be calm.*

"It is Lord Fang," whispers Eighth Daughter. "Great heavens! What can he want? He is one of the Empress's closest advisors, you know. He writes poetry for her."

Down in the courtyard, Autumn Moon and Swiftarrow step from the shadows. The horseman, this Lord Fang, jumps a little at the sight of them. Eighth Daughter grins. Just as I'm about to ask her what this night-time meeting is all about, the horseman dismounts in a flurry of silk robes. Even from this distance, it is clear he has taken too much wine.

Swiftarrow's spirit-horse is strong and bright with misery; I taste the bitterness of his sorrow from here. Why does he care so deeply? What hold does this Lord Fang have over him?

"So what is he here for?" I whisper.

Eighth Daughter opens her mouth to answer but then stays silent to hear what is being said.

"He's talking in a lot of flowery palace speech, but he says that Swiftarrow behaved very badly at court—" Eighth Daughter whispers, hurriedly; she lets out a gasp— "and that he went off without begging the Empress's leave – he says it's lucky she chose to be amused. But *he* was not."

"What is it to do with him, anyway?" I begin, swept up in the mystery of it all even though I don't care three mares' teeth what happens to Swiftarrow. "What is Lord Fang—"

"She is not one of your slaves," Swiftarrow snaps, down in the yard, "so do not speak to my mistress as if she were."

Lord Fang strikes him across the face with the back of his hand.

Eighth Daughter and I both gasp. Why did he not dodge the blow? Even I could have done so. Autumn Moon lays one hand on Swiftarrow's shoulder.

Lord Fang speaks, again so quickly that I cannot make out the words.

"Oh! He says that he has come to take what is his!" Eighth Daughter whispers.

"Is Lord Fang Swiftarrow's *father*?" I hiss back.

Eighth Daughter turns to stare at me. "Didn't you know that? I thought everyone did."

I understand Swiftarrow's reply perfectly. "No," he says. "I do beg your pardon, Lord Fang, but no."

And, as we watch, Lord Fang steps closer so there is barely a finger's width between them. I can feel the heat of his rage from here. Swiftarrow does not move, and I have to squash a flicker of respect for his courage.

"Fang Shiyu, you will learn to obey me." Lord Fang speaks with slow, icy fury.

Swiftarrow spits on the ground. "I am not Fang Shiyu."

Before our eyes, he steps sideways into the shadows cast by the courtyard shrine and is gone. He has faded into the night.

"Heavens," whispers Eighth Daughter. "Great heavens."

Without another word, Lord Fang turns his back on Autumn Moon, mounts the gelding and rides away out of the gate.

Autumn Moon stands alone in the courtyard, watching him go. Eighth Daughter grabs my arm. "Duck!" she hisses, and we huddle beneath the windowsill. "I do not think we were meant to see that."

I could not agree more.

Beyond the walls of the Forbidden Garden, the twelfth bell has just rung across the city. I lie awake in the moonlight, listening to Eighth Daughter's slow, steady breathing. Poor child. She cried a lake of tears, wailing that she would never see Swiftarrow again after his wicked father had come to take him away.

"And he just ran off," she sobbed. "Don't you see, Asena? Lord Fang is a cruel man. If Swiftarrow is ever caught, Lord Fang could easily have him strangled, and no one would punish him for it."

I cannot sleep, even though I know soon we must all rise for meditation in the hall, many hours before the rest of Chang'an wakes. Every time I close my eyes, I see Swiftarrow – and Baba. Swiftarrow's father is cruel and a drunk. Baba is lost to me for ever, but when I was born, he held me in the palm of his hand like a new kit and such was his joy that he wept. What a fine daughter I grew into – so befuddled by the beauty of a half-bred T'ang boy that I let him send my people to their deaths. I mustn't think about Baba and Mama. I'm never going to see them again. But I know what Mama would say to me now. I can almost hear her voice. *Admit it, Asena: you feel pity for the boy because his father is a heartless lout.* It's true. Never mind everything Swiftarrow has done, I am sorry that he burned with such misery when Lord Fang rode into our courtyard.

Wait. Our *courtyard? Am I starting to become Shaolin?* I might still see Swiftarrow's spirit-horse, but I am no true shaman any more, not without my wolf-guide. So what am I? Shaman or Shaolin?

A deeper darkness falls across the chamber. Has a cloud

drifted across the moon? No. There is someone here with me and Eighth Daughter. Someone else. I sit up, mouth dry with fear. What I would not give now to be holding a knife—

"I did not come to hurt you." It is Swiftarrow.

Heart pounding, I stare straight ahead, not meeting his eyes.

He has not spoken to me since the Blind Trial – nor I to him. He steps away from the window, crouches at my side, an arm's length away. "Asena, please hear me. Please don't pretend I am not here."

It is the first time I have ever heard him speak my name. I look up and I wish I had not, because the sight of his face still whisks the breath from my lungs. His lip is cut, clotted with dried blood, slightly swollen.

"You should hold a warm compress to that." I speak before I can stop myself. Once a healer, always a healer. "What do you want?" My voice is sharp and bitter, louder than I'd meant.

Eighth Daughter murmurs in her sleep, shifts in her tangle of sheets. Swiftarrow and I both freeze. At last, she breathes steadily again, soundly wrapped in sleep.

"I am sorry about the Gathering," Swiftarrow says, quietly. "Truly I am. And I'm sorry for taking you away from your kin—"

"What's left of them," I hiss, wishing that my words could burn him.

"When I found you, there was a man at your side,

wounded in his leg. He called your name as I took you away—" Swiftarrow falls silent, looking as if he wishes he had not spoken.

I stare at him. Could it have been Baba? Could it?

"What did he look like?" *Oh, Baba.*

Swiftarrow shrugs. "He was tall, with his hair in many plaits."

Baba and Uncle Taspar were the tallest of all our kin, and I know my uncle died at the Gathering because I saw his corpse next to Shemi's. Could my father really still be alive? I will never see him again, but perhaps Mama will.

Swiftarrow is watching my face – I feel the heat of his gaze – he's waiting for me to speak.

"Am I meant to be indebted to you now that I know not every last man in my family was butchered?" I demand, voice shaking. "Why are you telling me this – do you think it makes all well again? That it strikes out what you did?"

He does not deserve to see how grateful I am for this small, unsteady flame of hope.

"I am sorry," he replies, angry now. "I thought it might offer you comfort."

"Nothing you can say will ever comfort me."

He sighs, making an effort to control his anger. "Listen: I am leaving, and you will not have to look upon me any more. But I give you my word: I shall never betray the Horse Tribes again. I swear it. I wanted you to know."

"What you do is none of my concern," I reply. My eyes are burning but I will not let him see me cry. "If it's forgiveness you seek, I can never forgive you for betraying the Gathering, because I have no mercy on myself for letting you do it. I do forgive you for taking me away from my father. It was no more than I deserved."

"Asena, do not blame yourself—"

"But I must." Raw heat spreads across my face, and I am glad that it is dark. I would die of shame if Swiftarrow knew how his green eyes and golden skin had scrambled my wits.

"I am sorry," he says, again. He waits for a reply, but I give none. I say nothing, looking past him to the moonlit window. Swiftarrow tore me away from my father's side, and now he must leave his home. It is a fair bargain. But as he slips across the chamber, back to the open window, fast and fleet as a cat, I find myself wishing that he would not go. Despite everything he has done, I still wish he would not go.

21

Swiftarrow
In the House of Golden Butterflies,
a few days later

On his knees, Swiftarrow bowed so low his head rested on the reed matting. It smelled of dust, of summer's heat. Rain hammered against the shutters; he was relieved to get away from it. The roads were running with water, the ditches full. His hair was wet: the maids had forced him into a bath and then a dry robe, fussing and shaking their heads over his own sodden, street-mired clothes. How strange to be wearing embroidered blue linen instead of Shaolin black. This morning he had awoken before dawn, as if he were still in the Forbidden Garden and not sleeping in the stable-straw behind Madam Ha's tavern. But he could not return to the temple: he had no wish to bring down the wrath of Lord Fang on Autumn Moon. *My old life is over.* Never again would he spar with Red Falcon in the courtyard: scorpion, wolf, swallow, dragon. There would be no more laughing with

Hano in the cook-room, no more catch-ball with Eighth Daughter in the hall.

And no more Asena.

"Little brother, you need not kneel." His sister White Swan sat cross-legged on the couch, bright in her robe of fire-coloured silk, hair hanging loose around her shoulders like a spill of ink. "Come and talk to me." She sounded serene as ever, but that signified nothing. A drunken man might very easily choke the life from a concubine who had displeased him and meet with no more than a fine: in the House of Golden Butterflies, hiding one's true feelings could mean the difference between life and death. Swift-arrow pushed the thought from his mind and sat at her side. His sister kissed both sides of his face. Her breath was sweet with the scent of cloves.

"Tea, O brother?" White Swan leaned over to the table and poured two cups, handing one to him.

Swiftarrow took it, forgetting to thank her as he gazed out of the window. An autumn-red plum leaf drifted by, and he sighed. What was Asena doing now? *Glad I am gone, most likely.*

"Our father is a dangerous man, Swiftarrow," White Swan said, quietly. "You would be wiser not to persist with this disobedience."

He jumped, splashing tea over the borrowed robe. So she did know. She stared at him, one eyebrow raised at his clumsiness.

"What is her name?"

Swiftarrow looked up. "What are you talking of?"

"Come, brother, where are your wits?" White Swan sighed. "Whenever men act with such foolishness, one can safely wager there is a girl at the back of it. Who is she?"

"I cannot set one foot beneath the roof of Lord Fang, and that is all," Swiftarrow replied. First Autumn Moon and now White Swan. Why were all women so wretchedly knowing?

His sister frowned. "Truly you have hidden yourself well these last few days. Have you not heard?"

"Heard what?" Swiftarrow demanded. "Say."

White Swan turned, gazing out of the window. The sky was grey with gathering rain. "Lady Fang is dead. The summer fever took her to the ancestors four nights ago. Lord Fang is now in mourning."

"What has that to do with us?"

"She left him only daughters. And it would seem that the same was true of his concubines. Save our mother, who bore you." White Swan smiled. "Swiftarrow, you are Lord Fang's only son. If you had any sense at all, you would befriend him now rather than whipping the man into a fury by speaking to him with plain disrespect and then refusing to come when he called."

"I care nothing for being his only son. I want none of his gold."

"Come, we both know you are not speaking the truth – it is not riches you seek but Lord Fang himself. Your father."

"Do you claim to know my mind better than I? I hate him."

"You wish you did," White Swan said. "It is not the same. Listen to me, Swiftarrow. Go to our father as he has asked, yet I warn you he is not what you long for him to be. Take great care. Speak to him with respect, beg his forgiveness, but remember that a cat cannot be a dog. Lord Fang will never change."

"Why should I beg *his* forgiveness?" Unable to look at her any longer, Swiftarrow went to the window, staring out at the garden. Lily-flowers floated on the pool's surface like pale fists. He remembered his mother lying in her chamber, bathed in rosewater, clad in grave-clothes, a lump of pale green jade in her mouth. *They are burning Mama's things in the courtyard,* White Swan had told him, holding his hand. *They are sending her best robes up to Heaven.* The smoke had scorched the back of his throat, clung to his hair. The House of Golden Butterflies had rung with mourning cries, but Lord Fang had wept silently the morning after his most beloved concubine died, standing on the bridge, looking down at the lilies.

Will he take us away when he goes? Swiftarrow had asked that day, watching him from the window.

And White Swan had replied, *I do not think so.*

"You must beg forgiveness because he is your father," she said, "but that is not the only reason: people are beginning to talk. The feud between Lord Fang and his wrong-side-of-the-sheets son has become quite the delicious piece of gossip. Is this really a wise time to draw curious eyes to yourself, Fang Shiyu?"

"Don't call me that," Swiftarrow hissed, and then asked, "What do you mean?"

White Swan smiled. "But Fang Shiyu is your name – one of them. There is nothing you can do to alter the fact. Accept it. Come, Swiftarrow. Do you think I am a fool? What reason had you to be in the palace? Do not tell me the Empress summoned you there to give thanks for that poor barbarian girl."

"I was following orders when I took her—"

"I do not doubt it, and more than likely with my life as forfeit to make sure you succeeded," White Swan interrupted. "What manner of dangerous little errands are you running for Her Imperial Majesty now?"

"O sister, don't speak her name with such contempt," Swiftarrow said. "If the wrong person were to hear, you would be dead by morning. Listen, the Empress has ordered me to spy on our dear uncle, Lord Ishbal."

White Swan frowned. "It's well known that the Empress has lost trust in the Tribes, even Ishbal, who claims loyalty to her. She is terrified that they will all rise up against the Empire once more."

"It is time the Horse Tribes were free of the Empire's claws. I will spy on Ishbal's camp, but I mean to find out how many of his men agree with me. Together, the Tribes shall defend themselves. Apart, they will be defeated."

"Swiftarrow, attempt no such thing!" White Swan hissed. "It is purest treachery to the throne. If you were discovered—"

"I have betrayed the Horse Tribes once. General Li ambushed their camp and so many died. I cannot do such a thing again."

She shook her head. "I know. I did hear of it, and I wept. I know it's wrong that you must serve the Empress, carrying out her dreadful commands. But, brother, if you are caught double-dealing, she will have you gutted like a pig."

"I will not get caught." He smiled at her. "Come, you know I will never be caught."

She sighed. "I could not bear it. Truly, I could not."

"You will not have to. Did you see Brother Red Falcon last ten-night, when you went to hear the sutra?"

"Yes. We listened to it in the meadow, and it rained." She paused. "Snake-eye has still not returned from the temple at Mount Shaoshi?"

Swiftarrow shook his head. "No. But surely the Abbot will grant Autumn Moon leave to take us east. And when he does, we can all be free of Chang'an, and free of the Empress."

"Until Snake-eye returns safely, we can never be at ease. If the Empress heard the Shaolin were making ready to leave her, she would have every last one of you strangled in the market-square. Do not forget it. Swiftarrow, spy on Lord Ishbal if you must and play a double-game if I cannot stop you – but please take care. At least give the gossips nothing more to discuss."

Swiftarrow did not reply. What was the use in swearing an oath he could not keep?

22

Asena
Somewhere in the Entertainment Ward, several days later

I climb the earthen rampart that loops around the Chief Moneyer's hall, crouching low. There's a smell of stale oiled silk and spices: the moneyer likes fine things and has spiced cinnabar-paste rubbed into the carved window-lattices so that the air within is always scented. I long for the wide-open freshness of the Horse Tribe ridings, but I must not think about what I cannot have, or I will forget my task. It is my first, so I want to do it well.

Go to the House of Golden Butterflies, Autumn Moon told me at dawn. *Seek out the courtesan White Swan. Last night she danced for the Persian ambassador, and the Empress wants to know what he said to her, addled by drink and beauty. She suspects he doesn't speak of his king's true intentions at court.*

Me? I said. *I am to go?*

Autumn Moon smiled, but her eyes were shadowed. *You are ready, little Shaolin.*

I suppose she must make the best of what she has got now Swiftarrow is gone.

The Entertainment Ward spreads out below me, teeming with folk. They are like maggots swarming through old meat. Chang'an may be my prison, but I will never grow tired of watching it. I stand in the shadows a moment, gathering my wits. I've never been in this part of the ward before, and if I'm not to get lost I must keep my mind on the way.

I wonder if I will see him: Swiftarrow. Or has he left the city altogether?

In the market, they say that Lord Fang has gone mad with grief and rage, Eighth Daughter whispered at me as we broke our fast this morning. *The jackass-merchant told the fish-trader that Lord Fang plays music each night to Lady Fang's corpse hoping that she will get up and dance with him. And there is a reward of a thousand coins for anyone who can deliver Swiftarrow to the guard, and Lord Fang has sworn to cut his throat when he is found!*

Red Falcon told her not to pass on such witless gossip, and Eighth Daughter started to cry. *But I am afraid for him,* she cried.

Do not be, child, Red Falcon said, patting her on the shoulder. *Swiftarrow will look to his own safety. I just hope he has found some peace.*

I must put him from my mind and think about what Autumn Moon has asked me to do. *Keep your mind on the task.*

* * *

I'm in the market now. In Chang'an, I can hardly take two steps without finding myself among another throng of stalls selling all manner of stuff – bales of low-grade silk, cook-pots, lamp-oil, sacks of ground wheat-flour and jars of wine. I weave past a crowd gathered at a dumpling-stall. Then there's a fortune-teller on his stool next to a man selling live eels in buckets. But none of this is what I seek. I'm getting closer, though. The air grows heavy with the scent of many perfumes mingling on the wind. I cannot be far from the House of Golden Butterflies now, jewel of the Entertainment Ward, home to the Flowers of the T'ang.

I dodge a greasy peddler selling oil from a vat hanging around his neck and walk quickly north, keeping to the side of the road near the ditch, close to the line of cherry trees planted by some long-dead emperor as a gift to the people of Chang'an. I have never seen a courtesan at close hand before, only glimpsed them being handed out of palanquins at the gates of the Daming Palace or seen a flutter of bright silk melting into a dark doorway. I'd feel safer if only my wolf-guide were here at my side, but I'm afraid he really is gone for good. Yesterday, I tried to leave my body and let my spirit fly above Chang'an so that I could see how to reach the Entertainment Ward, but I could not do it.

I can't worry about that now, either. I must be mindful of my task, or I will fail.

Running along in the shadows behind a row of stalls,

I come to a high earthen wall. There are peach trees here, and late-flowering peony bushes breathing out their scent, just as Eighth Daughter had told me there would be. I pass the gate, not missing the two guardsmen posted on the other side: I can't see them, but I hear their heartbeats so I know they are here, even though both are dozing now in the late-afternoon sun. I shall leave them in peace: it is not my plan to enter the House of Golden Butterflies by the door with the guards' blessing. No: I come from the Temple of the Forbidden Garden, so I come in secret.

Stepping swiftly behind a peach tree, I crouch at the base of the wall, looking up. It's not far to climb, no higher than the peach tree itself. The tail-end of the summer was glaring hot; the packed mud has cracked and not been repaired. Good for footholds, but too dusty, too dangerous. The last thing I want is to bring the whole wall down on top of me. That's no way to gain an audience with White Swan – though what I'm to do when I find her, I've no idea. Eighth Daughter is full of amazement about how much T'ang she is able to stuff into my head with each day that passes – but there are still so many words I do not know. How am I to talk with White Swan?

Up the peach tree I go, and I can look down on the market stalls now. The women keeping them are talking idly over their shoulders, always with one eye on their wares. Thieves are many in Chang'an: I saw one beaten by the Gold Bird Guard in the East Ward not long ago. If I'm spotted slithering up this tree and over the wall, I'll be taken for a thief myself. But I'll not be seen: Autumn Moon has taught me how to move even softer, even more shadow-like than I could before.

I heave myself up to a higher branch, the highest one that can bear my weight: I feel it bounce like a bowstring. The wall's top is just out of arm's reach. I must leap for it and pray to Mother Earth I do not go tumbling down, for I would land right on the flour-seller, who is now scratching her head. Very likely she has lice.

I stand, clutching the top of the trunk. Peach-bark digs through the soles of my thin sandals. *Don't look down.* I steady myself. *There is only the wall, nowhere else to land.* I leap. Yes! I land in a crouch, fingers digging into sandy, hard-packed mud. I hear rushing water and look down on a small stream winding through a grove of bamboo: the House of Golden Butterflies has a garden close on as fair as the palace's. But there's no time to linger.

Now I'm within the main courtyard. I see a hall half hidden by a shrine and a stand of mulberry trees. *Oh! There's someone—* A girl younger than me with hair cut straight across her forehead stands halfway up a frame of lashed-together bamboo, stripping mulberry leaves to feed the silkworms.

Don't look at me, girl; I'm not here.

I must move. Sooner or later, some quick-eyed person will spot me, and I shall have failed my first task. Keeping close to the rustling forest of bamboo, I run up to the hall. Windows, windows, all latticed, screened with oiled silk. The one I want is slightly ajar. Taking care to breathe slow and steady as Autumn Moon has taught me, I creep closer and run my hands over the wooden window-hinge. It will either stick or creak, or both, if I open the window any wider. But I'm ready. I reach for the bag at my belt and dig my fingers inside, pulling out the small clay flask of hemp-oil Autumn Moon gave me. I didn't know the words to ask her what it was for, but now I see, and I silently thank her. Standing on the tips of my toes, I oil first the topmost hinge, then the bottom one.

Ah—

Someone is within. The door clicks shut, someone breathes softly; silk rustles as they move. A rich, warm scent drifts out at me: cloves and herbs and peonies in full flower. I hear a hollow clink – the lid of a clay pot being lifted and set down again – and a woman humming to herself.

Gently, gently, I rise up and peer over the window ledge into the chamber. The woman sits facing away from me. She reaches up, pulling combs from her hair till it hangs down her back in a smooth black curtain. The sleeves of her sky-blue robe are so wide they brush the floor. The warm, heady smell of cloves and peonies grows stronger whenever she moves. The breath catches in my throat. Is this her? Is this the famed White Swan?

I touch the window-lattice lightly with one finger; it swings open wider, soundless. Now I must be soundless, too. I listen to the drumming of my heart and breathe deep, slowing the beat as Autumn Moon taught me. *What's to be afraid of? Easy, Asena, easy.* Leaning on the windowsill, I push down, leaping up light, and now I'm in, crouching on the floor. The woman's back is still turned, but I hear footsteps: someone else is coming. A maidservant?

There's a wooden chest three paces away from me. *Don't turn around, courtesan, whoever you are.* I duck behind the chest; it smells of cedar trees. Now even if she turns around, I shan't be seen. *Are you White Swan,* I wonder, *or some other Golden Butterfly using her chamber?* I hear footfalls coming closer. The woman sits still on her stool, waiting. The stool is carved of dark wood, inlaid with the pale green stones they call jade.

A girl comes in wearing a plain white robe: some kind of maidservant. The woman looks up, hair rippling down her back, and they speak so fast I can't follow. The maid does say "my lady White Swan" though, so at least I know I'm in the right place.

Yes! I have done it.

All I've to do now is wait. The maid bows her head and takes up a comb. Oh, I pray she is not about to start weaving one of those great towering piles of coiled hair rich women wear. I will be trapped here till I'm frozen with cramp. Autumn Moon is the child of a nobleman, and she told Eighth Daughter and me that her mother would spend half a day having her hair twisted, woven and stuck with pins. Autumn Moon jokes that it is why she took her vows and joined the Shaolin, for now she has no hair at all—

What was that? A silvery flash of light near the woman's

159

left shoulder. *There it is again.* The maid goes on with her task as if nothing has happened.

It is a spirit-horse.

Very faint, she is, barely there: a shadow. But all the same, White Swan has a spirit-horse. So Horse Tribe blood flows through her veins, too. This is why Autumn Moon sent me.

And what is *that*? Did I just see the faintest golden shimmer at her shoulder, like a newly kindled flame? It's gone. I stare. I am weary from waking each day before dawn to meditate in the hall, my belly hollow as a nutshell because the Shaolin never eat past noon; my eyes are tired. I am seeing what is not there.

My thighs start to ache, crouching in such a way, but I must not move: if I make the slightest sound, they'll hear me. All it will take is that maidservant checking behind this chest for a bamboo-rat and I shall have betrayed myself.

White Swan's spirit-horse moves again: I make out the curve of her withers, the flash of a tail. All of a sudden, she steps forward, leaping away from White Swan, just a silvery shadow in the air like a splash of falling water. *White Swan's spirit-horse has seen mine. No, no: I am not here.* But it's too late. White Swan sits very still and stops her flow of talk with the maid, holding up one slim, pale hand. Her spirit-horse skitters back to her side, and I sense its confusion. It's sure there was another spirit-horse here, but now I've drawn mine in close to my body, and I think of nothing, only deep, soft blackness as Autumn Moon taught me.

"Go," White Swan says to the girl in T'ang, and then

something else so fast I can't make it out. The girl nods, smiling, and bows her way out of the room. White Swan is a good liar: it's clear the maidservant suspects nothing. As soon as the girl has gone, White Swan is on her feet in a rustle of sweeping silk, quietly dropping the door-latch so no one can get in. She turns and I see why this woman is the most prized of the Golden Butterflies: her face is smooth and lovely, even without the colours T'ang women rub into their cheeks and lips. She's afraid, though: her lips are pressed tight together and she's breathing quicker. She steps into the middle of the chamber.

"Well," she says, "where are you, then? I know you are here, Shaolin. I have been waiting."

I've not much choice: I stand up, walking out from behind the chest. White Swan jumps a little, then smiles at me, eyebrows raised.

What is so special about White Swan, this courtesan? How is she able to see what others don't?

For a short while, she simply stares at me, and I at her.

At last, she speaks. "So you are the Horse Tribe girl my little brother netted in Samarkand."

White Swan is Swiftarrow's sister? I bow to hide my shock.

She smiles. "Yes; indeed, Swiftarrow is my brother. I will tell you the story: Mama was a courtesan. When our esteemed father heard that she was dead, he flew into a rage. He is a fine poet, but at that time he needed to look upon Mama's beauty in order to write. Mama was meant to dance for him the night she died. Father thought her death inconsiderate and threw a porcelain statue of the Enlightened One at the wall, breaking a screen painted by the Empress's own cousin. It was quite the scandal. So I remained here to dance, repaying my mother's debt, and Swiftarrow was given to the Shaolin to atone for the broken statue."

I stare at White Swan's beautiful, calm face, but in my mind I see only Swiftarrow. Does having Lord Fang for a father excuse the deaths he caused?

"So I must own that it is my fault you are here, and that your kinsmen died," White Swan goes on. "The truth is: Her Imperial Majesty named my life as the price Swiftarrow must pay if he failed the task. I wish he had paid that price – my life is scarcely worth the loss of so many – but he did not."

I stare at her, unable to speak.

"So," White Swan continues, "do not be too harsh in your judgement of my brother."

"Nothing can excuse him, or—"

"And, for that matter, do not be so harsh on yourself, either." White Swan's eyes seem to burn me. "You are very young to—" She pauses. "We all do wrong at times. Perhaps young people more so, without experience to guide them."

I stare at her, frozen with sudden fear. I feel as if all my most secret thoughts are laid bare before her. But she does not know the truth of it. I was not just any young girl, giddy and raw-headed. I am shaman, or at least I was, and I had a duty to my people – to care for them and guide their spirits.

Instead, I chose not to tell my kin that White Swan's pretty brother followed me that day in Samarkand. I led him straight to the Gathering: a foolish mistake that even a child of six summers would not make.

"I do not understand," I say at last, desperate to turn the flow of talk elsewhere. "The Empress has Horse Tribe fighters in her army, yet how did your mother's kin come to be in Chang'an?"

White Swan raises an eyebrow. "Autumn Moon must have been keeping you close by her side, child. Have you never been to the city wall in the Eastern Quarter? Go there and you'll learn something new. The Tribes are scattered further than you, a girl stolen from so far in the west, might suppose."

Somewhere close, I hear the thud of a closing door. There is not much time.

"Autumn Moon sends me to learn what news you had of the Persian ambassador when last he came to your chamber." The words come out in a rush.

White Swan sighs. "Tell her it is as we expected it should be: the King of Persia says we shall have the finest of the plants, but really they keep the best for themselves, sending our beloved Empress only the inferior ones."

"The finest of what plants?" I ask, before I can stop myself. I am meant to be on my way back to the Forbidden Garden already.

She smiles. "The less you know, little Shaolin, the safer you will be. But in this case it can do you no harm to learn that the King of Persia possesses the secrets of a flowering plant called indigo: it dyes cloth the finest, deepest blue – brighter and richer than the sky. The Empress longs for her gardeners to grow the stuff themselves so she need not send her courtiers to spend so much cash in the Persian market each fall-of-the-leaf."

I hear footfalls coming closer.

"Go," White Swan tells me, "and tread carefully among the Shaolin, Horse Tribe girl." She smiles, but there's an odd, shadowed look in her eyes as she turns away, back to her mirror of polished bronze, back to her curtain of shining hair and the painting of her face.

Once outside, I crouch beneath the window, listening to the door opening and closing, White Swan speaking kindly to her maidservant. I did it: I can move without being seen. I can take on the spirit of tiger, wolf, swallow, scorpion. I am Shaolin. I cannot help smiling. Autumn Moon does not know it yet, but she has taught me how to kill the Empress: silently. I will come for the Empress quiet as a ghost, but I will kill her as a Horse Tribe girl – with my knife, and her eyes shall be open to see it coming.

With each day that my skills swell, I am a step closer to revenge, the Empress a step closer to her death. And hand-in-hand with the Empress's death, there awaits my own.

I must be away from the House of Golden Butterflies; I could still fail in my task if someone spotted me here. But White Swan has a spirit-horse. I long for another sight of it. Softly, softly, I rise up on my knees till I can see over the windowsill. White Swan sits facing away from me as a maid-servant in white robes combs out her shining river of black hair.

White Swan's spirit-horse is nowhere to be seen. Moments slide by as I wait for a glimpse of it, but there is nothing. Unease settles over me like a cold wet blanket laid across my shoulders. First it was so faint, so shadowy, and now it has gone, faded to nothing. Her spirit is weak, broken. What great wrong has she committed?

It's none of your concern, I tell myself. If I don't get away from here now I shall be caught.

Back in the garden, I slink through the forest of bamboo, moving fast. I do not like this House of Golden Butterflies. I want to get as far from it as I can, and from the concubine inside who sees my most hidden thoughts as if they were painted on my face. But as I run, my heart sings: the Empress will die by my own hand; she will pay.

I have chosen my path.

I cannot go back.

I can only go on.

23

Swiftarrow
Fang Shiyu

He knew the way. Flags emblazoned with Lord Fang's name were mounted on lances outside the gate, but Swiftarrow did not need to read them. He had been here before, many times. Just to look. This close to the Xingqing Palace, the streets were full of Gold Bird Guards. He kept out of their sight. Lord Fang employed his own men to guard the homestead but they did not see Swiftarrow walk past the shadow-wall outside the main gate, built to keep evil spirits from passing through into the courtyard. *Your shadow-wall is not enough to stop me, O Father.* Swiftarrow swarmed straight up the gate, dropping down to land in the main courtyard. The white-clad maid who ran by was blind to him, too, hurrying in from the rain. She disappeared into the cook-room; the door slammed shut behind her. Lord Fang was well known for granting his servants the liberty to wear a yellow or red tunic beneath the death-white commoners' robes they all hated so much. But it was not so today.

So it is true, Swiftarrow thought: *Lady Fang is dead.* If the gods had chosen differently, she would have been as a mother to him. Would she have been a kind stepmother, or a cruel one? But fortune had turned another way, and Lord Fang's wife meant nothing to him. Nor did her tribe of daughters, not one of whom he had ever met and who, if the market talk were true, lived out their days in a country manor house thirty days' ride to the south because their moon-faced lack of beauty bored Lord Fang out of his wits.

My half-sisters, Swiftarrow thought.

He paused outside the weather-worn cedar door. Standing in this place of death, the clamour of Chang'an seemed far away – the braying of a jackass whipped along the road, the chatter of folk waiting to hear the masked fortune-teller who plied his trade beneath a drooping willow tree at the street corner, shrieking children. Making sure he remained unseen, Swiftarrow waited in the courtyard of his father's house, listening. He heard the low chatter of servants, the clink of a clay spoon against a pot, a distant zither playing "Mournful Summer of the Fading Peony."

Music in a house of mourning? A crime punishable by beating and exile. Swiftarrow swallowed his shock. It was clear Lord Fang chose to believe he lived above the law's reach. *And maybe he does.* Following the sound, Swiftarrow opened the door. Once inside, he paused, looking around. Another white-clad servant ran by, but she did not see him, even though she passed so close that the breeze she stirred up stroked Swiftarrow's face. She was gone, closing the door behind her. In the hall, the windows were all shuttered, and it was dark. He smelled the freshness of clean rushes on the floor. At the far end, an oil lamp glimmered at the feet of a gold-wrought statue: the Enlightened One, sitting peaceful and calm.

I will be calm, too, Swiftarrow swore. *I will not step from the Path of Peace for the sake of Lord Fang.* He chased the music, running quick and quiet through the darkened hall. At last, he came to another door. When he laid his hands against it, he felt the coolness of jade tiles inlaid into the wood.

This might have been my home: our home, White Swan's and mine.

Behind the door, the zither played on. "Fading Peony" drew to an end and another song began, one Swiftarrow had not heard before. It would be easy to go in unseen, keeping to the shadows. But this time, he did not want to. He pushed the door. It was unlocked and swung open before him.

The music stopped.

The chamber was in half darkness, lit only by a single lamp resting on a table scattered with flasks and jars. Rolled-up scrolls were stacked on every table, even the windowsills, blocking the light: a library. The sour smell of wine hit the back of Swiftarrow's throat, sickening him. Clad in robes of mourning white, Lord Fang was sprawled on a wooden couch strewn with tiger-skins and bolts of heavy silk. His hair was loose about his shoulders, long, grey-streaked. The girl sitting at his side wore nothing save the peacock feathers in her hair, clutching the zither as she stared at Swiftarrow, mouth half open.

Lord Fang took a sip from the silver cup in his hand. "My dear girl," he said, "get out of my sight. Cannot you see how my son will look at nothing but the floor?"

Swiftarrow glanced away as the naked concubine walked past, still holding her zither. The door closed behind her with a slight creak. He had sensed her watching him. It was just past noon and in the marketplace gossip would spread faster than a fever. *Before sunset the whole of Chang'an will know I am here. White Swan can stop her worrying.*

He dropped to his knees, bowing low, letting his forehead rest against the fresh rushes on the floor.

"Get up."

Swiftarrow sat back on his heels, head bowed.

"So, it pleases you to grace my home at last." Lord Fang spoke with such cold rage that Swiftarrow had to crush a glimmer of fear.

Swiftarrow met his eyes. "I only wish to serve my esteemed father in whatever manner he deems best." *What can he do to you? Nothing.*

"Enough. Let us be clear with one another," Lord Fang said with quiet menace. "It seems I must begin to rule you. I beg you, know this: nothing means more to me than the good name of the House of Fang; I will have neither my honour nor the safety of my innocent daughters put at risk by a foolhardy brat I left behind in a whorehouse. Yet you are Shaolin: you move faster than thought. I cannot control you in the manner of most fathers. Therefore why did you allow me to strike your face last time we met?"

It is as if he saw into my mind. Swiftarrow paused a moment before replying: his father was clearly not only an arrogant man but a shrewd and ruthless one. He would need to be handled carefully. Swiftarrow chose to give him the truth.

"Because I am not much afraid of you, my lord."

"And you wanted me to know it." Lord Fang smiled, eyes cold. "So what was a rebuke from me becomes a little lesson from you. Perhaps we are not so different after all. But remember this: I will find a way of punishing you, Swiftarrow, should you choose to annoy me again."

Swiftarrow looked up at his father. "I do not doubt it." He thought of that long-ago meeting with the Empress, when she had bidden him cross the western desert with General Li. *Believe me, boy,* she had said, *life as a courtesan is full of danger.* Lord Fang had stood by then, saying nothing to defend White Swan. Would he go so far as to threaten her, too?

I don't know him well enough to tell. He would have to watch, and wait, and learn.

"Good," Lord Fang said. "I am glad that we have reached an understanding. Now leave me. Go to the hall and bid one of the servants show you to your chamber. Remain there until you are sent for. There is much to discuss."

"Yes, my lord." Swiftarrow got to his feet and bowed his head. *I will play your little game for now, O Father.*

He had reached the door when Lord Fang spoke again. "Twenty years," he said, quietly. "Twenty years she was at my side, and now she is gone, her corpse packed in ice, waiting to be buried. Our little lives are too short, and it is so cruel."

Swiftarrow stood still, hand resting on the door. It was not what he had expected to hear.

Lord Fang looked up, face twisted with anguish. "Go!" he hissed.

The eighth bell rang across Chang'an, and Swiftarrow sat cross-legged on a couch bestrewn with leopard hides, facing his father across the table. Lamps flickered, casting long shadows over porcelain bowls of fragrant spiced meat and steaming rice. All lay untouched.

"Eat. It is not my intention to starve you." Lord Fang drained his cup of wine and poured another. The jug had been painted with dragons and twisting vines by a well-taught but unskilled hand. Swiftarrow wondered if it was the work of Lady Fang.

"I beg you to excuse me: I am forbidden to touch food after midday."

"Temple rules do not apply in this house," Lord Fang replied. "But do as you will. Have you been spying on your mother's kin as Her Imperial Majesty commanded?"

"The Shaolin never speak of a task before it is done with, sir."

Lord Fang nodded, slowly. "Very well, but remember

this: you and your sister mean nothing to the Horse Tribes. Beware of the one who calls himself their leader, this Lord Ishbal. He may be your kinsman, but he is not to be trusted. Spy on him as the Empress has ordered, but do not be drawn in by the barbarians. They are not loyal – even to their own kind."

"You need not warn me." Swiftarrow stared across the table at his father. "My grandfather sent Mother to the Emperor as a gift. He was happy to let his own child spend her life pleasing any man who had enough gold. Therefore his son is hardly a man I wish to trust." It was a satisfying blow, and Swiftarrow had waited many long years to strike it.

Lord Fang put down his cup. It hit the table top with a soft click. "Tell me," he said; "what is the name of that barbarian girl at the Blind Trial? The one you captured in the west. She had a great deal of spirit. When you caught her at the end, the entire court thought you were going to kiss her. I hope she does not meet with any danger, running errands for the Empress."

It was a threat.

"You will have to spin a love-tale about someone else, O lord. Girls are forbidden to me, Father, so I try not to pay them too much heed. But I still would not wish Asena any harm. I have done her enough already."

"So pious, child." Lord Fang laughed, with what sounded like genuine amusement.

Swiftarrow glared at him. "Someone is coming." He listened to the footfalls growing louder. Lord Fang might have won the skirmish, but the battle was still undecided.

"A servant," Lord Fang said. "Well, it seems you have been granted a reprieve from this line of questioning. Wait."

A round-bellied man came in, clothed in bone-white robes of mourning. He bowed. "Your lordship, have you all that is required? More meat? I take the liberty of remarking that Cook has roasted the deers' tongues exquisitely well."

Lord Fang waved him away. "No, Jin. That will be all."

Swiftarrow was surprised to see the fat servant bow again and begin to speak. He was truly concerned at seeing the untasted food. "You must eat, master. Starving yourself won't bring her back."

"Enough, Jin."

"What of the young master?" Jin asked, undeterred by Lord Fang's chilly reply: either he was a courageous man, or Lord Fang a kinder master than Swiftarrow had supposed. He did not miss the edge of disapproval and scorn in Jin's voice, though, and realized he was not meant to. *I am the child of a mere concubine in a house grieving for a wife.* And clearly she had been a well-loved mistress.

Lord Fang sighed. "That will be all, Jin. In future, ensure that my devoutly religious son has the repast he needs before noon. Now go: I wish to be disturbed no more."

Jin bowed his way out of the room, and Lord Fang did not speak again until the sound of his footsteps had faded.

"Jin's family have served this house for five generations. His father served mine; he serves me." Lord Fang shook his head. "And yet, in these damnable times, no one is to be trusted, and most particularly not one's servants, nor those of one's friends."

"Yes, your lordship," Swiftarrow said, quietly.

"Speaking of loyalty, remember that you do not belong to the Tribes," Lord Fang went on. "When you visit Lord Ishbal's camp, I trust, Swiftarrow, that a misguided sense of kinship will not lead you to anything that would bring disgrace upon this house. Swear to me that you serve only the Empress."

Swiftarrow met his father's eyes. "I swear it."

"I pray," said Lord Fang, "that you are not foolish enough to lie."

And Swiftarrow said, "Of course not."

24

Asena

I crouch atop the wall, ready to leap. The Forbidden Garden spreads out below me, a tangle of shadowy trees and whispering bamboo stirred by the night breeze.

The Tribes are scattered further than you, a girl stolen from so far in the west, might suppose.

White Swan told me to go to the city wall in the Eastern Quarter.

Glancing over my shoulder, I catch sight of the moat, silvery in the moonlight. I shiver in my wet clothes, shuddering at the memory of long waterweeds tangling between my toes as I swam. I did it, though: I got out without rousing Eighth Daughter, who is always so restless and talks in her sleep. I crossed the shadowy great hall, barely stirring the silken drapes as I passed (though Red Falcon's painted wolves and tigers did seem to watch me, somehow).

I land in the alley, barefoot, breathless. *The jump was*

further than I thought. But I've not hurt myself, at least. If I'm found out here with a shattered ankle bone there will be trouble. I glance up at the sky, shivering. It's a clear, cold night. I would have given my right hand for a way across the moat without swimming, but I dared not cross the bridge. It is Red Falcon's turn to guard it this night, and I'm not fool enough to think I'd get past him.

The lamps in the marketplace still burn, throwing out pools of buttery light, but most folk are at home, warming themselves by the fire. Only the foolish and the desperate venture out in cold like this after the eighth bell. I leave behind the raised voices and walk till I'm away from the market, keeping to the shadows.

I skirt the southern wall of the West Palace. My wet hair sends trails of ice-cold water down my back. A man in a hooded cloak hurries by carrying a basket full of squawking chickens. The streets here are thick with Gold Bird Guards: gangs of armed men marching about to keep the peace. *Time to start running again. I must be quick. What if Eighth Daughter wakes and finds me gone? Will she think I've gone to use the privy, or will she wait and see if I come back?*

There is little sense in fretting over that now.

I run, darting from shadow to shadow, thinking of nothing save the shadows themselves. I am one with the darkness, one with the streets: no one can see me.

I smell standing water and here it is, beyond the road-side ditch, behind a line of leafless pear trees: the canal. Red Falcon told me it had been made to bring wheat into the city by water. If I follow the canal to the east, I'll come to the Xingqing Palace and, at last, to the east wall of the city.

Lamp-lit boats work their way west towards the palace warehouses, and I hear low voices, even a woman singing softly as I pass the nearest boat. They've a fire alight on-board; I smell hot broth and frying meat. A family living on the water. *Oh, how I wish I were in the saddle, riding with Shadow back to camp, guided by bright fire-glow in tent doorways and the scent of smoke. But that will never happen again.*

I hear the flapping of silk flags again, more than I can count. *When I round this corner, the wall of the Xingqing Palace shall rise up before me. Here we are.* The hall's tiled roof juts out above the wall. Leaving the palace at my back, I run south past a row of old silk warehouses. They're guarded, of course, but that's no matter: I've no business with silk-thieves. The East Market's on my left, closing up for the night now. Lamps are going out all along Ironmonger's Row. The night's alive with clattering and shouting, and there's a small crowd gathering around the fires by the East Market pond. Someone is selling hot wine.

At last, I reach the wall of Chang'an: a great mound of earth, towering far above my head. Easy to climb. There's a tangle of mulberry trees here, good cover. There are people talking nearby but I can't quite make out the words: *curse it!* More guards. It's a gate, closed now for the night, but guarded still. Four men lounge around a fire flickering in an iron bowl.

"Feel's like rain's on the way," one says, wrapping a heavy

cloak tight about his shoulders. "I don't like this clammy air. Always gives me a pain in the shoulder, it does."

"Best have another drink, then, friend."

They pass around a cup of steaming ale. *I'm not here, O guardsmen, you can't see me.* I'm tired of climbing walls this night. Maybe I should just go out by the gate? What a fine test of my skills. If Autumn Moon knew about it, she would be proud. I grin to myself in the darkness: if Autumn Moon knew what I was doing now— But she does not know. *None of them will ever find out.*

I smell kumis. I smell it for the first time since the Gathering, all those moons ago. The T'ang do not drink kumis: just ale, wine and tea.

This can only mean one thing: *there are tribesfolk near here, and lots of them.*

My head's afire. Are they friends or enemies? With the Empress or against her? What are they doing so close to the city? At the Gathering, a man said he'd heard rumours some of the eastern Tribes were loyal to the T'ang – but never did I think to find a camp rammed against the walls of Chang'an. I must get on the other side of that gate. Letting out a long breath, I run closer, burning with the thrill of it: the gate-guards must be able to see me now – I'm only an arm's length from the nearest one. *But they just don't.* I could go anywhere, I could do anything and no one would be able to stop me.

Closer, closer. I smell the guards' breath – they have all been eating spiced pig-meat. The stink of ale hangs about them like a cloud. *I'm not here, I'm not here; don't look at me.*

This gate is latched from the inside with a heavy bar. Without a sound, I lift it – it's heavier than I thought. One of the gate-guards has started to hum a marketplace song, out of tune. But they've still not seen me, and now they shan't. I push the gate softly, softly, making a gap just large enough for me to slip through. That's it: I'm out. I'm out of the Forbidden Garden and out of Chang'an.

Behind me, the gate-guards begin to argue over who left the latch up.

"I thought I heard something," one of them says, and I freeze where I stand, just in the lee of the great city wall. There's movement, footfalls; they're getting up to have a look around.

"Nothing." The other voice is scornful. "You grow right wary of shadows, friend."

I hear a soft thud as they close the gate, a clank as the latch is drawn down, and I smile in the darkness.

Fools.

I turn towards the light, and now I see what White Swan was talking about, out here beyond the city walls. I do not only see it; I smell it: a swathe of tents, pale like mushrooms in the moonlight, dotted with firelight, and the sharp, sour-milky scent of kumis heating above campfire flames. I hear voices, words I understand, all flowing together smoothly like a river, so smooth and easy; it is not like trying to unravel the speech of the T'ang. "Bring that water over, friend" ... "Did you see how my brother went with the new yearlings?" ... "Are you hungry, my dear?" ... "Curse your eyes:

that's my drink you've kicked over" … "Pour yourself another then" … "Come, see what I did with that bridle."

I must make sure to stay hidden in the shadows: I'm wearing T'ang clothes and these folk shall know me as a stranger.
The warm sweetness of horses drifts on the wind: here they
are, tethered among a stand of dusty, stunted trees near one
of the streams that passes through the east wall and feeds
the canal in Chang'an. Most of the horse-kind are sleeping
but some are not, and I taste the colour of their minds, the
shape of their thoughts: the coolness of river-water, the hissing rush of wind through branches. There's a hot flicker of
wariness; a mare turns to look at me, and I reach out with
my mind, calming the horses.

I'm one of you. Be easy, my dears.

At least I still have this skill, even though I have not seen
my wolf-spirit for day upon day, night upon night, and I
cannot leave my body any more. *Oh, Shadow.* My face is wet
with tears. Where is he now?

I leave the horse-kind behind, coming closer to the cluster
of tents. Squatting down by the trunk of a mulberry tree, I
watch, breath caught in my throat. A stout woman ducks out
of her tent, a deerskin-wrapped baby strapped to her back.
She's holding a flask and dips a finger into the neck, flicking milky-white kumis to the north, south, east and west,
making her offering to the spirits before everyone drinks.

I stare in horror: *she has no spirit-horse.*

She stops and looks up at the cloud-smeared night sky
before ducking inside again, and I hear her saying to some

unseen companion, "There's rain coming before dawn, you may be sure of it."

What could she have done to wound her soul so dreadfully? She looked so fat and kind. And the baby? He had no spirit-horse, either.

A strange, cold feeling sits about my shoulders. There is something wrong with this camp, with these people. Why are they here in the shadow of Chang'an when all anyone can talk of up and down the Road, and even within the city itself, is the Empress's longing to crush the Tribes and turn us all into wall-dwellers?

A baby with no spirit-horse – how could he have so badly wounded his soul? He cannot even stand on his own two feet.

A gaggle of children squat by a fire a few paces away. Again, no spirit-horses: children and babies with no souls. They are poking twigs into the flames, whispering amongst each other, giggling. I shiver. I must go closer. I want to wander among the tents. I want to smell the night-meat brewing, and listen to talk of horse-kind and hunting.

What are they doing here? What are they doing clustering about the walls of Chang'an, these broken, soulless people?

Keeping my head down, I slip past a group of men with long, braided hair talking in voices so low I can scarce hear what they're saying. They have no spirit-horses either. They pass me in a wave of stale kumis-breath. They've come from a tent much larger than all the others: it must take half a day to get the frame up. Why would anyone bother, only to take it all down at the next shift of camp? A man stoops on his way out of the huge tent, striding off to piss among a stand of spindly trees, and I see the glow of firelight coming from within before the tent-flap swings down again after him. Thick white clouds curl from the smoke-let in the roof, coiling up towards the night. The wondrous thing about a tent is that it has no true walls, and any fool can listen to what's being said inside. All I need to do is wait.

I've been crouching so long my legs feel as if they are on fire. But I cannot make myself move: just listening to the river of Horse Tribe voices coming from within the great tent is like drinking sweet water after weeks in the desert. There must be a great crowd of folk in there – I hear the thundering beat of their hearts and it sounds like a herd of horses galloping across hard ground; one moment I snatch a thread of talk about someone's young son and his first day in the saddle, the next someone else is speaking all hushed about a woman, and now there's a burst of laughter. Another person quite near where I crouch is talking about the rising cost of silk coming out of Chang'an and how the merchants further down the roads aren't much liking it. All the while, I smell the sharp kick of hot kumis, and every now and then, I catch the scent of mutton cooked over the fire. My mouth fills with spit: oh, how I long to eat good food again.

"Hush yourselves," calls a rough voice. "The Highest One speaks, Son of the Sky Father, Lord of the Horse Tribes."

A quick, hot thrill runs through my body, right down to

my bare toes. *Son of the Sky Father? Lord of the Horse Tribes? What man dares make such claims?*

Quiet falls within the tent till I hear nothing but men drawing breath and the pounding of their hearts. The sounds of the camp around me seem louder now: a dropped iron pot clanging on hard ground, the cry of a fretful child.

"Men, your lord Ishbal speaks. It has come to our ears that the Horse Tribes of the west have been caught up by rebellion."

Lord Ishbal. I've heard that name before. Where?

There's a burst of muttering among the gathered men, louder, of course, among those closest to me.

"Well, of course they were? Did he not send men to fight them?" I hear someone say. "I don't know why we stay crouched up against the city walls like a motherless lamb looking for a teat to suck, not when there's the whole of the steppe to roam."

"Because our fathers came here, that's why, and they were not fools: sometimes it's best to stay close by your enemy. Better to have him in sight than not."

A hush falls, and that so-called Son of the Sky Father speaks once again: "Our kinsmen in the west have been unwise. Hearing of our noble Empress's desire to bring justice to the Roads they met in a Gathering a handful of moons back, hot with talk of rebellion—"

The Gathering. At the back of my mind, I see the running children, the woman lying face-down in her own blood. I see Shemi, dead, killed with no weapon in his hands.

Stop thinking of it. Stop it.

That's where I had heard the name: by the talk-fire at the Gathering: *Lord Ishbal has become the Empress's pet? Come, that can't be true.*

But it *is* true.

"Now, more than ever, we must prove our loyalty to the Empress." Lord Ishbal lifts his voice – oh, how I'd like to get a look at him. Traitor. "Soon the time will come to hunt down those foolish enough to resist her might. In return for our safety these last twenty years, the Palace asks for our help. We will join with the Empress's army and ride west. We shall find those of our kind foolish enough to resist and wipe them from the face of the earth that the Horse Tribes may never be shamed again."

I can't breathe. I pay no more heed to the rumble of voices within the tent now. General Li's half-breeds at least had T'ang mothers or fathers, no clan to call their own. This is much worse: tribe plotting against tribe. *Filthy cowards.* They should be white-hot with rage over the massacre at the Gathering: the lives of their own people were stolen, their corpses left to rot with none of the rites, their souls left to wander with no shaman to guide them to the World Below. And yet this Lord Ishbal is planning to ride out against his own kind.

I lean forwards on my hands, fighting the urge to be sick. My head spins: I'm dizzy. What am I going to do?

Did White Swan hope I would hear talk like this when she told me to come? What was she trying to tell me? I must go to her, back to the House of Golden Butterflies. Is she trying to stir up rebellion? White Swan and Swiftarrow – two half-bred children abandoned by their T'ang father. Reason enough for White Swan to hate the Empire. Wait.

There is someone here. They crash into me, pushing me to the ground, knocking the wind out of me. Choking, lying breathless on my back outside the tent, I feel cold steel at my throat. I can't see who has me – I'm caught by the Running Wolf trick, helpless with my shoulders and legs pinned to the ground. It's another Shaolin – it has to be – but who? I catch my breath at last. Who is it? They conceal themselves too well. Red Falcon? Hano again? Was I followed tonight? I am gripped hard by the wrists, knees digging into my thighs, and it hurts so much. All the T'ang words I know fly from my mind like swallows fleeing an eagle. I still hear fires crackling away in the camp, folk moving around, making ready for sleep, a man whistling – I wager he's on his way back to the tent after checking his horse-folk one last time. All those people, going about their lives, not knowing I'm about to die out here.

I'm not fool enough to cry for help.

"Please stop!" I whisper in my own tongue. "Please!"

"You."

It is Swiftarrow. He gets up, hauling me to my feet, dragging me away from the tent.

"What are you doing out here?" Each word falls from his lips like a cold stone. "It is not safe. Did Autumn Moon send you?" His eyes are narrowed into glittering slits. He is truly angry.

I stare at him: his spirit-horse has gone. What terrible thing has he done to kill his own soul? Or are my powers spilling out of me like rice from a split sack?

"I might ask the same of you," I hiss at last, wrenching my arm from his slackened grip. "You swore to me that you would never betray the Tribes again, yet here you are spying for the Empress! What are you planning now? Did you not hear what that filthy traitor in there said? How many innocent children will die this time?" Tears spring to my eyes and I turn away, not wanting him to see.

"Did you truly think it was so simple?" Swiftarrow demands, furiously. "Wicked T'ang hunting down the free and noble Horse Tribes? Don't be a fool. Lord Ishbal's folk have served the Empress these last twenty years and been well paid for it, too."

"It is wrong."

"Ah, everything is so easy for you," he hisses. "Right and wrong are as different as gold and mud. In the time of our grandfathers, the Horse Tribes looted and burned every trader-inn they could find, every T'ang city. How many innocent folk lost their lives then, do you think?" He turns and spits on the ground. "Things are scarcely ever as they seem, Asena—"

"Who's there?"

We both freeze at the cry, turning in the same instant. A woman holding a bucket stands less than twenty paces away.

"Is anyone there? Hie! Hie! Rani, is that you? What are

you doing there? Rani? Who is there?" The woman's voice lifts, edged with fear. If we don't get away from here now, Swiftarrow and I will both be caught by the traitor Lord Ishbal.

Without another word, without a sound, we run.

25

Asena
The next morning

It is cold in this chamber. Red Falcon has lit the black iron brazier but its flames wink at me from the other side of the room, far from the open shutters I sit beneath. Eighth Daughter and I sit very still, hunched over the low table, eyes fixed on our work.

We are learning the art of making false beasts.

It is a strange kind of magic. I gaze down the length of the chamber at the banner hanging from the furthest roof-beam. It is covered with writhing animals, birds in flight, all painted by Red Falcon. But when I dip my brush at last into the pot of black ink, I make nothing but a meaningless smudge on the silk. I think of Shadow, and how we used to gallop together across the grasslands at sundown, my hands gripping his pale mane. Yet it is no use: my memory of him won't flow down the paintbrush. My mind is crowded with what I saw and heard last night. I shall never forget what

Lord Ishbal said. His words rattle about in my skull like pebbles shaken in a dish:

Soon the time will come to hunt down those foolish enough to resist the Empress's might. We will join with her army and ride west. We shall find those of our kind foolish enough to resist and wipe them from the face of the earth that we may never be shamed again.

What am I to do? Why did Swiftarrow lie? Why bother swearing to me he would not betray the tribes again when it's clear he is? If Swiftarrow and White Swan have kin among Lord Ishbal's clan, I suppose he might have been visiting them. Yet why slither around outside the tent like that? It does not tally. I can't stop thinking about his spirit-horse: gone. Utterly vanished. What does it mean? We scrambled up and over the city wall side by side, but the moment my feet touched the street, I saw no more of him. Very likely, he had no more wish to be caught by the Gold Birds than I.

Just as I was starting to believe that Swiftarrow is less rotten-hearted than I thought, I have been proved wrong. Once again, I hear Mama's voice as if she were next to me: *Why are you so disappointed, my girl? You know he is a rotten apple. Why wish him otherwise?*

Never mind Swiftarrow, I must find a way of stopping Lord Ishbal.

Red Falcon stands only a hand span away, gazing out of the window at the shaded pools and secret corners of the Forbidden Garden. Like all Shaolin, when at rest Red Falcon scarcely moves at all. He doesn't even twitch a finger. What does he see in the world that I cannot? I will never find such peace.

Helpless, I stare at the pale square of silk spread out before me. Someone has come in: the chamber has grown a heartbeat warmer with the heat of another body. I peer sideways from the tail of my eye: it is Autumn Moon, speaking very fast and quiet to Red Falcon. She is looking at me, and so is Red Falcon. Eighth Daughter glances across at me, a question in her eyes. I shrug, just a tiny lift of my shoulders. *I don't know.*

Have they found out where I went last night?

I look away. I don't want Eighth Daughter drawn into a mess of my making. Autumn Moon turns from Red Falcon and looks at me. "Come," she says. She is riled about something, and I pray she has not found out where I was.

Autumn Moon walks so fast I must run to keep up with her. I sift through my head for the right T'ang words. It's much harder to speak than it is to understand. "Why me? Where to?" I ask her.

Autumn Moon shakes her head. "I do not know why," she says, sharply, "but the Empress wants you."

I stare at her, frozen to the ground. On the far side of the courtyard, silk banners flutter and flap and the creatures painted on them seem to move of their own will: pouncing tiger, leaping monkey.

"You do right to be afraid," Autumn Moon says. "Ah, the Shaolin should never have come to Chang'an: we should have stayed well away from this place. Come –

since we are the Empress's playthings, we must obey her summons."

She opens the gate and I follow her through it.

My blood burns with the thrill of it, hotter than a draught of fiery kumis searing down my throat on a winter night. Revenge is in my sight like the deer fleeing a hunter in the forest.

The Empress has invited death into her chamber.

My forehead rests against the wooden floor as I bow, kneeling before an empty stool: the Empress has not even graced the room, and yet Autumn Moon and I must abase ourselves on the floor like worms. The smell hits the back of my throat, and I have to steady my breathing as if I were meditating in the courtyard, otherwise I shall be sick. It's a mingled reek of ancient, oiled cedar floorboards and camphor.

What was that? Footfalls on a creaking wooden floor. Someone approaches the chamber. Still on my knees and bowing low, I see nothing but the grain of the polished wooden floor, but I can hear Autumn Moon breathing beside me and the steady drumming of her heartbeat. I take courage from her stillness.

Has the Empress found out that I was creeping around the camp? Am I to be punished? Surely such a matter would be far below the Empress's concern. What can she want with me?

Don't be such a coward, girl, I tell myself. *It makes no difference what the Empress wants. How are you going to kill her?*

I am a fool: I ought to have made some excuse to Autumn Moon and gone to the cook-room for one of Hano's knives. A little knife would have been easy to tuck into the wide silk belt of my trousers, hidden beneath my tunic. If I leapt for the Empress like a tiger, I doubt Autumn Moon would stop me. But killing Her Imperial Majesty shall be no easy task. This chamber is surrounded with hidden guards betrayed to me by the sound of their breathing. One of them even breaks wind. They will cut my throat without thinking twice about it, and I don't want to be stopped before I have succeeded.

Now I know of Lord Ishbal's treachery, it is more important than ever to kill her. The Empress's death will send a crack running through the Empire, breaking it open like a barrel of rotten salt pork. Hordes of Imperial sons, daughters, nephews and nieces will swarm through this palace like maggots, poisoning, stabbing, accusing, betraying, all battling for the favour of a weak, bed-bound Emperor. Then no one will have a thought to spare for the Roads, and the Horse Tribes shall be left alone to ride the steppe. Mama and Aunt Zaka will be safe from the Imperial army, even if I never see them again.

How long are we to wait? I can't help thinking of a tale Eighth Daughter told me as we swept the courtyard eight nights ago: Lady Wu Deng was married to the Empress's middle brother. Lord Wu Deng was convicted of treason and his head cut off with a sword beneath the willow tree in the marketplace. Lady Wu Deng pleaded her innocence, a claim most of the court could well believe, given that she lived most of her life breeding long-tailed goldfish at her home in the country, twenty days' ride from Chang'an. But Lady Wu Deng starved to death in a bamboo cage kept in a grove of cherry trees within this very palace. They said the Empress showed great mercy, Eighth Daughter told me, because Lady Wu Deng was able to watch cherry blossom falling from the trees as she died.

So, yes, I am afraid.

Wait, what's this? Footsteps. *The Empress is coming.* The door opens and closes; cold air rushes across the floor: I feel it even through my padded winter tunic. There's a slight scraping sound as her weight drops on to the stool – she's not a heavy woman. I expected to hear the whisper of embroidered robes but I didn't: she must be lightly clad. She has come alone, too. No advisors, no gaggle of chattering courtiers, just the Empress herself.

She speaks a word I don't know – her voice is low, quite easy on the ear – and I feel Autumn Moon's light touch on my forearm. We are to rise. I sit back on my heels, head still bowed. Low, wintery sunlight slants in through the open shutters, glancing off Autumn Moon's shaven head.

"So we meet again, Horse Tribe girl." The Empress sounds as if she is close to laughter. "The barbarian child who runs faster than a deer and moves quieter than a shadow." *Is she mocking me?* "Has she done well?"

Autumn Moon bows, palms pressed together. "Your Majesty, Asena's mind is unquiet and restless: she has not yet found the peace true Shaolin seek." She shrugs. "However, her other skills are excellent, especially for one so late in coming to us. Most join the temple much earlier in life."

"Look at me, child." The Empress speaks so softly, so gently, but if I were to disobey I'd be dead before sunset. She has the power of a god. What was that tale I heard about her, back on the Roads? The Empress commanded her garden to flower in the first month of the year, when all was frozen and cold mist hung on the air. By morning, the peonies had opened.

I am afraid of the hatred uncoiling within me: if I look at this woman I shall fly at her and choke the life from her body. Not yet, not yet. There are too many guards.

Still staring at the floor, at the swirling grain of the cedar boards, I draw in a long breath and release it. Finding calm, I look up.

The Empress is just like anyone I might meet in the marketplace. Her face is doughy, but the hands resting in her lap are thin, the fingers delicate and whiter than maggots. Her lips and cheeks are not stained red, but her eyebrows have been shaven and painted in much higher so that she looks forever surprised. Her hair is drawn up into a knot. She wears a very plain robe, but it is the colour of fire and I never saw such cloth even in the marketplaces of Samarkand: it's as if the palace seamstresses have tugged reams of the stuff from the sun's heart. My heart's yammering so loud they must be able to hear. Autumn Moon nods at me: I must abase myself again now that I have been marked out for special attention. I bow low, forehead touching the floor, and sit back on my heels, trying not to let the hatred I feel show in my face.

"So, you have trained well, Horse Tribe girl. That is good." The Empress smiles. Her teeth are blackened: they must be full of rot. "How sad that you will always look like a barbarian, no matter how long you live among civilized people. So tall!" She shakes her head as if she is truly sorry for me. "However, child, I perceive that barbarians are not without their uses. Did you know that some of your kind make their nests outside the walls of our noble Imperial city, just like bears in the forest?"

A cold chill streams down my back – it feels as though someone has just poured a pail of icy water over me. *Does she know where I was last night?*

The best lie is always closest to the truth: "I had heard talk of it, O Imperial Majesty." I try not to show my anger, for she speaks as if the Horse Tribes are beasts, not truly men and women. I would not mind being reborn into the body of a bear when this life is over: bears are brave and powerful. But it's clear the Empress considers living like an animal shameful. I should like to snatch a handful of that fire-coloured robe and shake those rotten teeth out of her head.

The Empress smiles, treating me to another glimpse of her teeth. Aunt Zaka would say she ought to chew hard cheese to make them white and strong. "For a generation, those barbarians have been loyal to the Empire, but of late my husband and I have been given reason to doubt them.

What would you do, girl, in our place?"

Another cold splash of fear soaks through me. The Empress knows everything. Her eyes burn into me: can she see into my mind?

My mouth is dry. What am I to say? I glance at Autumn Moon: she sits stiller than a jade statue, her face calm. *Help me.* No one speaks a word; the Empress is smiling. I hear the guards' breathing quicken as they talk soft to one another about a woman one of them met in the leather-market. Outside, wind sings through the garden, whispering through the bamboo, rustling leafless branches.

The Empress taps one maggot-white finger against her knee. She is waiting.

I draw in a long breath. "I am not so wise as Your Imperial Majesty. I am only a foolish girl. Is not the punishment for treason death? Would the tribe outside your walls risk losing their lives?" May Mother Earth forgive the lie I am about to tell: "I am sorry to admit it, Your Majesty, but my people do not value honour. The Tribes will always act to save their own skins. I think it unlikely they shall betray you."

"I do hope you are right." The Empress speaks very softly. She almost sounds kind, but I know she starves innocent people to death in cages. It was on her orders that so many died at the Gathering. The lives of men and women mean nothing to her: she will crush anyone she chooses as if she does but step on a worm. The Empress smiles. "But hope is not enough, little barbarian girl. My husband is a cautious man, and I know he would rather be certain that your people remain loyal." She laughs delicately. "You have learned the way of the Shaolin: I wish you to go into the barbarian camp and be my eyes and ears. Listen in on their talk and then spill their words into my lap. After all, I cannot go there myself."

Cannot she hear the pounding of my heart?

The Empress turns her gaze on Autumn Moon. "Do you permit this?"

Autumn Moon has no choice. "I grant consent, Your Majesty."

I can no longer escape the true reason Swiftarrow was in Lord Ishbal's camp. He is spying on the Tribes for the Empress, despite his pledge to me. There can be no doubt, no other possible explanation. And, as I've been given the same task, it's clear the Empress does not trust either of us.

A gush of cold air pours into the chamber through the window-lattice, bringing with it the scent of cinnabar-paste and wood-smoke. Outside, the sky is whiter than the belly-feather of a goose. Rain begins to fall.

My eyes burn with unshed tears, but I shall not weep till I am alone. I don't care for the danger we are both in, Swiftarrow and I. Even though it does not matter, because I will kill the Empress and be killed myself, his treachery has cut me open and flayed the skin from my body. I am raw with pain and I will never find peace.

26

Swiftarrow
Pagoda of the Great Wild Goose,
Temple of Maternal Grace

The sun rose on the ninth morning of the ninth moon and a red glow stained the sky above Chang'an. *Like blood mixing with well-water,* Swiftarrow thought. All was quiet. The Wild Goose pagoda rose up behind him, reaching to the sky like a great spear of bamboo. Crouching at its foot, he leaned back against the crumbling bricks, listening. The holy men of the temple were still at fast-break: he could hear their low, comfortable talk from across the courtyard, the soft clatter of eating-sticks against earthenware bowls. He longed for the Forbidden Garden where Hano would be serving broth with noodles. But there was no use mourning what could not be helped. The sweetness of chrysanthemum flowers stewing in hot ale drifted across the courtyard from a cook-room hidden among a jumble of temple halls, ready for the festival. On the far side of the courtyard, someone had left bronze basins full of bright chrysanthemums in neat rows, ready to be laid out in honour of the Emperor and Empress. The flowers glowed like suns, so bright even long past the end of summer: light within the darkness of winter to come.

At the sound of far-off hoofbeats, Swiftarrow sat stiller than a cat about to pounce and watched the gateway. Moments passed, and Lord Fang rode in, still clad in robes of death white. Swiftarrow stood, allowing himself to be seen, and Lord Fang dismounted.

"Bring water," Lord Fang said. The faint scent of last night's wine hung about him still. Swiftarrow knelt, scooping chrysanthemums from the nearest bowl so his father's mare could slake her thirst. Her flanks shone with sweat. Swiftarrow shook the water from his hands, droplets bright like pearls in the early morning light, pulled off his headscarf and rubbed the mare down with it. When he closed his eyes, he saw Asena.

"The Xingqing gate was open as I passed: the Empress will soon be here." Lord Fang offered no thanks for the water. "So," he went on, "the palace gossips tell me your little barbarian girl is also spying on Lord Ishbal's camp. Can she be trusted?"

Swiftarrow shook his head. "Of course not. It was senseless of the Empress to send her. Even so, have no fear about the girl, O Father: I will make sure she does no harm."

"Will you?" Lord Fang frowned. "The Empress's arrogance grows by the hour. She has become foolish. You and I are now players in a deadly game, Fang Shiyu. I shall turn my mind to our next move. In the meantime, by sending the girl after you to spy on Ishbal, Her Gracious Majesty has made it clear that she does not trust either of us. We must take care. Go home, Swiftarrow. Be as a son of the House of Fang, loyal only to the Palace."

"I beg your leave to attend the festival, O Father. Three ten-nights since, I swore to my little temple sister that I would take her."

Lord Fang was already mounting up. Once in the saddle, he turned. "Go then, if you will. So kind-hearted," he said, mocking. "Oh, I do not deserve such a son."

Swiftarrow watched his father ride out of the courtyard, away from the Temple of Maternal Grace. *Yes, you do*, he thought. *Oh, yes, you do.*

27

Asena
Later that morning

I open my eyes after morning meditation to find Eighth Daughter sitting at my feet, wrapped in a faded jacket belonging to Autumn Moon. The sleeves hang down over her hands.

"Asena!" She giggles. "It's the festival this day! No training, no painting, no chores. We will be allowed to watch the parade. We might even see the Empress. Come, let's break our fast and go, or we shall miss the best of it. There'll be hot pastries and chrysanthemum ale."

My eyes are sticky with the tears I shed before sleep came last night and those I shed at dawn before meditation. Grief settles over me once more but I smile, not wanting to cloud Eighth Daughter's joy. I wish White Swan had never told me Swiftarrow betrayed the Gathering because her life was the price if he failed. Just as I began to think better of him, he spied on the Tribes again after swearing not to. I might have followed the Empress's orders and gone sneaking to Ishbal's camp just as Swiftarrow did, but I don't mean to tell her anything. And if White Swan is still under threat, why bother to make a promise to me at all, knowing he could not keep it?

What a fool he must think I am, sweetening me up with honeyed words, telling me that there was a chance Baba might still live. Is this all just a jest to him, a game?

And yet he was so angry when he found me outside Ishbal's tent. *It is not safe,* he said. Why does he even care? Most likely he is furious because the Empress does not trust him to spy on the Tribes alone.

Drifting like a ghost, I follow Eighth Daughter out into the courtyard. It smells of fresh-fallen rain and salty mushroom broth. Red Falcon and fat Hano are already sitting at the rough-hewn wooden tables outside the cook-room, talking softly as they dip eating-sticks into their bowls. Autumn Moon is at the shrine beneath the mulberry tree, shaking a droplet of soup from the end of her eating-stick: an offering to the gods and to our ancestors. I go to fill my bowl from Hano's iron pot and feel as though I walk through the web of a spider, trapped by strands of misery that slow down the sun's march across the sky.

If I am to stop Lord Ishbal, I can waste no more time. I must kill the Empress, and so myself. I wonder how her guards will do it? Will they cut my throat there and then, or shall I be taken in a cage to the market-square and strangled before a baying crowd?

Autumn Moon lays a hand on my shoulder and I look up from my untasted broth. "Are you well?" she asks, frowning.

I shrug. Hano and Red Falcon are watching me. Eighth Daughter is out in the courtyard turning somersaults; her empty bowl sits beside mine. How long have I been sitting here like this?

"Asena," Autumn Moon says, quietly. "I know it must cause you pain, being ordered to spy on your own kind. There is little else we can do but obey. Anger will not help anyone." She turns to look at Eighth Daughter, laughing in the courtyard, and I see what she is trying to tell me. Carrying out the Empress's commands is not all cowardice: if the Shaolin displease Her Majesty, she will make all of us suffer, including Eighth Daughter.

"Something must change," I reply. "It must."

"Asena, I do hope that you are not considering any foolish—"

"Don't worry," I say, trying to keep the bitterness from my voice: "I'll not do anything to bring down harm on the rest of you." I turn away, not looking at her and, at last, Autumn Moon sighs and walks away.

"Eat, little barbarian: you are all skin and bone," Hano calls, but the kindness of his smile does nothing to warm my misery. I do not miss the look passing between Red Falcon and Autumn Moon, either. I must try harder to seem content or I will be too closely watched to carry out my plan.

I stare out at the courtyard again and Swiftarrow is here,

stepping out of the shadows, holding out a flame-bright flower to Eighth Daughter. The golden sheen is fading from his skin with the passing of summer. He is pale, his hair deep black.

"Little temple-sister," he says, "I stole it for you."

Eighth Daughter shrieks with delight. "Where from? Where from?"

But Swiftarrow does not answer, just laughs and walks towards the cook-room, calling out to Autumn Moon, who steps forward to embrace him. Red Falcon slings his arm around Swiftarrow's shoulder, messing up his hair like a fond older brother. It is the rare smile on Swiftarrow's face that sets alight my anger: how dare he be so happy? Traitor. I cannot stop myself. The bench screeches across the flag-stones as I push it away from the table.

"Asena?" says Autumn Moon, but she can wait. Swift-arrow has stopped at the sight of me, drawing away from Red Falcon, now frozen. I am still holding my soup bowl. He does not move even when it flies from my hands and hits his shoulder, leaving a splash of cold mushroom broth on the floor. The bowl hits the flagstones, cracking neatly in two. Birds sing in the mulberry trees. A light wind cools my face.

"Nothing is as it seems, Asena!" The words fly from my lips. "You were right about that! You spy on the Tribes for that woman."

Eighth Daughter stares at us, mouth open.

"Be silent." Swiftarrow's voice is calm, cold. "The Shaolin

never speak of a task before it is complete: you have been told this, therefore why do you? Otherwise I would ask why *you* were in Ishbal's camp. Are you a traitor to your own kind?"

I leap at him in tiger-form, hands clawed. People are calling out, but I cannot hear what they are saying. Swiftarrow meets me as a wolf, pouncing, pinning me to the ground, and the flash of rage in his eyes makes me glad. As a wolf, I roll to one side, rejoicing in the strength Autumn Moon has taught me. We fight from one end of the courtyard to the other, whirling, gripping, lunging. We don't fight our own minds in search of peace, but each other, out of sheer fury. Light on his feet, Swiftarrow runs up a pillar and leaps at me from the sloping roof of the hall, dragon-form. In his anger, he is clumsy and knocks down a tile, which shatters on the ground. I meet him, pushing, ducking, afire with rage. We are both making mistakes. At last, he knocks me to the ground and, instead of twisting away like a snake, I fall heavily and there is a great burst of pain across the back of my head. I sink into darkness and just as quick I am hauled out of it by his voice.

"Forgive me. I am sorry—"

"You have both done quite enough." It is Autumn Moon. It is only the second time I have heard anger in her voice: the first was the night Lord Fang came. "Are you not ashamed to let Eighth Daughter witness such behaviour?"

I open my eyes. Red Falcon and Autumn Moon crouch at my side. Swiftarrow kneels, gripping my hand. I do not let go. Even after everything he has done, I want him to keep holding my hand.

"What is the meaning of this?" Autumn Moon demands. "Asena?" What riles her? The fight, or Swiftarrow holding my hand? Flushing, I tear mine away from his.

"Oh, do not speak to me of calm and peace and the Way while I am sent to spy on my own people, and you do nothing to stop it!" I snap. "It is all so false."

Autumn Moon turns to Red Falcon and Hano. "Has anyone told our sister Asena of the news we await?" she asks.

No one speaks. Autumn Moon nods. "Very well. Asena – go and lie down. We will talk of this when you are rested. Swiftarrow, come into the hall."

What news can this be? Red Falcon helps me to my feet. My head spins and I stumble. I have to lean on his arm as we walk inside. As we go, I turn and over my shoulder I see Swiftarrow still kneeling in the courtyard, and poor Eighth Daughter standing at his side. Hano will have to take her to the festival now. The unhappiness painted across her face completes my own.

I lie still, watching sunlight move across the wall. On the other side of the chamber, Eighth Daughter has left her covers in a tangle, hanging off the bed. If Mama were here, she would fold them, shaking her head. Tears stain my face and my head aches. The door swings open and I look up. There is no one in this city I want to see.

It is Swiftarrow.

Even now, my heart beats louder, faster just because he is near. I wish he would take my hand again. How foolish. After everything that has happened.

He closes the door. "I had no wish to hurt you. I am ashamed."

I still cannot see his spirit-horse.

"Leave me," I say. "Just go."

But Swiftarrow does not move. "Autumn Moon told you of Brother Snake-eye's journey to Mount Shaoshi?" he says. "If the Abbot permits, we shall all be free to leave Chang'an."

I sigh. He is not going to leave me alone. "She told me after she spoke to you. But in the meantime, we are still here. What have you told the Empress about Lord Ishbal's camp? You might think I'm a traitor to my own kind, but I'm not going to tell her anything."

"I should not have said that. I was angry. I know you have no choice but to go. I've told her nothing, either. Lord Fang speaks to the Empress on my behalf—"

"Your father."

He shrugs. "Fang is no father to me. I tell him nothing of any use. Listen, Asena—" he crouches by my bed— "we have both been spying on Ishbal's camp, and you must know as well as I that a good number of his men wish to rebel against the Empress. But what if Lord Ishbal himself could be persuaded to abandon his loyalty to the Palace, and stand side by side with the Tribes? We should act together, you and I, not against each other."

I glance out of the window to hide my shock. This was not what I expected to hear. "Why should I trust you?"

He sighs, sitting back on his heels. "I know I have done you nothing but wrong. Yet here is a chance to do good. Asena, I do not deserve your help, but what of the Tribes? I betrayed my own mother's people, and I have a duty to make amends."

I draw in a long breath. If Swiftarrow is lying, I would be wise to keep him within my sight. "How are we to persuade Lord Ishbal to do anything?" I demand. "Do you truly think a man like him would listen to you or me? In his eyes, we shall be nothing but a pair of young whelps barely worth looking at."

Swiftarrow smiles, and I care for nothing else. *Fool, fool – I am worse than a drunk, addled by his beauty.* But I need him. I need to keep watch over him because he cannot be trusted. If his spirit-horse is so faded I can no longer see it, what wickedness is he guilty of?

"My sister," he says. "Lord Ishbal and his men go to watch her dance at least every tenth night. White Swan will beg him to grant us an audience. And when my sister asks a favour of a man, he grants it."

I stare at him, my heart pounding. *So be it*, I think. *I will play your little game for now.*

28

Asena
In the House of Golden Butterflies

I cling to the roof-beam; it presses into my belly as I stare at the chamber beneath. Swiftarrow lies facing me and his hair hangs down, black like the wing of a crow. He is watching, too, stiller than a dried-out log in the grasslands that grows white in the sun, year after year.

Below us, a group of men sprawl on low couches set out around the walls, drinking hot wine. Some are clad in barbarian clothes – buckskin trousers, rough tunics. Ropes of twisted gold hang about their necks, around their wrists. One, a man with a thin hollow-cheeked face, has a missing hand and I wonder how he lost it. Even from up here in the roof-space I catch the lingering warm smell of horses that hangs about these men, and a tear slides hot down my cheek: I have not been on horseback since before the Gathering. Hardly daring to breathe, I wipe away my tear – should it catch the light or fall and strike the balding pate of the man just below me, someone might look up. The other men are T'ang. They wear the rich purple robes of high-class palace officials.

Girls with painted eyebrows and red-stained lips come in bearing flasks and dart about, pouring out more wine. From the waist up they are naked, shadows falling across their bare shoulders, their pale breasts. I stare at the skirts they wear, which are sewn with swathes of bright feathers and seem to change colour as the girls move from shadow to light. How many jewel-feathered birds were killed to make such things? The girls retreat and stand waiting to be summoned. A hush falls upon the chamber. I glance at Swiftarrow. He watches the room below, still, silent. His grip on the beam tightens and I look down.

White Swan is here. Clad in a robe stitched with winged snakes, she holds an unsheathed sword in each hand. Firelight glints off polished steel. A black river of hair pours down past her waist, falling forwards and tumbling across the tiled floor as she bows low.

Where is her spirit-horse? I still cannot see it. Not even the faintest flicker of silver. Cold fear thrashes in my belly, as if I have swallowed a live fish. First the tribe outside the city walls, Lord Ishbal's people, then Swiftarrow. Now White Swan. What have they all done?

Not one of them can be trusted.

The men whistle and clap, but it is as if she hears nothing at all; she does not even flinch. She raises both arms above her head; the swords flash. Pushing my distrust aside, I watch, breathless, as she dances. Lighter than the wind, she wheels and spins, black hair flying. The swords spin, too, flashing, falling. The men cheer and clap. Even the purple-robed courtiers cannot look away, and they have surely seen the sword dance countless times. The feather-clad girls stand watching. They must be chilled to the bone, but none make a sign of it save the smallest one. She is hardly more than a child, hair still cut in a blunt fringe across her forehead. She shivers and cowers as the older girls glare at her.

White Swan steps backwards into another deep bow, and just as I think the dance is over, she leaps like a deer and both swords fly upwards, hissing through the air. My heart hammers as each person in the chamber follows the flying swords with their eyes: we are going to be seen. *Think of nothing; be not here. Think of nothing and they shall not see you.* The blades seem to spin so slowly, flashing, glinting. A gasp rises up from the Horse Tribe men below and one of them lets out a ragged cheer. The swords fly higher, higher – White Swan must have the strength of a tiger in those slender arms. If I reached out now I could touch the nearest blade and my blood would fall like rain on those gathered below.

The swords fall, tumbling, turning. White Swan leaps again and catches each one by the handle, bows once more and sweeps out of the chamber, hair hanging loose and shining down her back. Below us, all the men save one break out in cheering and clapping.

I look up, right into Swiftarrow's face as he crouches like a monkey on the beam. He need not warn me: we must leave this chamber now or our luck will run out.

White Swan sits straight-backed on a jade stool, watching us. Her face is fair as ever, but her lips are pressed together. Is she angry or just afraid? Swiftarrow kneels at her feet; I crouch on the cedar chest I once hid behind, feeling as though I should be otherwhere.

"Did you see the man with one hand?" she asks. "That was Lord Ishbal. I know not what you may have learned listening to secrets in that camp, but after his fourteenth cup of wine this evening, our esteemed uncle told me that he longs to ride the Roads once more, to escape the shadow of Chang'an. So it seems you are in luck." She turns to Swiftarrow. "Ishbal might be our uncle but that hardly means we can trust him. Do not forget that his father – our grandfather – gave Mama to the Emperor as a gift: his own daughter."

"We will go to Ishbal anyway, O sister," Swiftarrow says, "with your help or without. All I say is that it shall be much easier to persuade him if he knows we are coming. You take the choice."

White Swan stares at him a moment. "Very well. Ishbal is waiting for me to dance again, and afterwards I will speak with him alone once more. He knows that his men are starting to bear doubts about the Empress. I shall ask if he will see one of you. Going together might make him feel hemmed in and put him on his guard. But I pray you will take care—"

"I will go, if it is to be one of us and not both," I say. "The Tribes are my people and I will save them."

"Don't be a fool. It is too dangerous. I must go," Swiftarrow replies, sharply.

"*You* brought me to the temple," I snap. What does he think I am, some hopelessly weak little maiden? "Autumn Moon has trained me well. I can easily manage this Lord Ishbal. If he turns against me, I will run."

Swiftarrow opens his mouth to answer, but White Swan holds up her hand, silencing him.

"Much as I dislike the whole of this plot, Asena is right. Swiftarrow, your face is a copy of our mother's. It has been many years since Lord Ishbal last laid eyes on his sister, but even so, he might see her in you and grow suspicious. I am only a woman, and so he does not fear me, but Ishbal is not likely to be foolish enough to think you mean him well."

Swiftarrow frowns, but nods. "I don't like it," he says. "But if it must be so—"

"I will manage," I say, daring him to deny it.

White Swan sighs. "I only pray that you will both take care."

Swiftarrow bows before her. She kisses his hand.

"Leave us, brother." White Swan turns to me. "I would like you to stay a while, Asena. My wish is to speak to you alone."

Swiftarrow looks at her, but she just meets his unspoken question with a smile. Quick as a cat, he turns, leaping for the window. I listen as the sound of his heartbeat fades.

"Don't fear: he has truly gone," White Swan says.

How does she know? She has never lived among the Shaolin; she can't hear what others do not as we can. *We*. I have become one of them; I am no longer just Asena of the Horse Tribes, Asena the shaman. I am Shaolin.

"I beg you, Asena, sit down." White Swan waves one hand at the carved wooden couch.

Another cold wave of fear rushes through my body from head to toe. I must turn my back on it. I must keep to the Way. I sit on the couch, crossing my legs; I watch her.

White Swan is no longer smiling but looking at me in that strange manner again. The back of my neck prickles. *It is as if she can see inside me.*

"My mother always told me I came into the world of men with two souls, Asena. One was a horse, she used to say; the other a wildcat."

I stare at her. She is like me. White Swan was born a shaman, too. So where is her spirit-horse? My heartbeat quickens. Sick dread rushes up my throat and I draw in a long, sharp breath.

"I have never been certain," White Swan goes on, "but I suppose it is why I see the souls of others, burning like silver fire, and why I read the secrets of men's hearts with such ease." She shakes her head. "And it is no gift but a curse."

"No," I say. It cannot be true. If White Swan were a shaman, I would be able to see this wildcat-spirit she speaks of, and her spirit-horse, too. Yet I see nothing, not even the faintest shadow. She is wicked. She has done a great wrong.

Or perhaps she has just lived too long among the T'ang, and now her spirits are locked up within her body.

And, anyway, she is lying. The T'ang have no spirit-horses, so how could she see what is not there?

But I know what she is about to say.

"Once, you had the spirit of a wolf as your guide, Asena, but now he is gone." White Swan speaks quietly. "And your spirit-horse is a twisted creature that limps and staggers. It grows weaker every time I lay eyes on you. Your soul is broken with the thirst for revenge and death. I am sorry, for it was my brother who brought you here."

I stare at her, breathless.

"And yet," White Swan goes on, "the holy people here say it is not others who create misfortune and misery, but ourselves."

In my mind, I hear the voice of Autumn Moon: *Keep to the Way, Asena, and you will be released from suffering. Turn your face from anger. Turn your face from bitterness.*

White Swan speaks softly, barely louder than the wind hissing through bamboo outside. "The great power in you is broken and twisted. The night before you first came here to learn my secrets, I dreamed of a she-wolf dying in a trap. The next morning brought you into the House of Golden Butterflies, Asena, and I saw the eyes of the wolf in yours."

"No," I say. "It is you. *You* have no spirit-horse. I saw it that first day, but it is gone now. So has Swiftarrow's. Not one of the people in Lord Ishbal's camp has a spirit-horse because they all betray the Tribes with their loyalty to the

Empress. Or maybe it is because they have camped so long outside Chang'an that they have turned into wall-dwellers."

White Swan shakes her head. "Even if you saw your closest kinsman now, Asena, you'd not see his soul. You let the power rot within you. You have betrayed yourself."

She is right. I hear Tulan's last words to me: *Your powers will remain strong only if you live by truth alone. Heed your wolf or lose him. Trust him. Never forget: the spirits only guide those willing to be led.* I did not live by truth alone. I lied to Baba about Swiftarrow. I refused to listen to my wolf.

And the truth is: I wanted Swiftarrow when I have known since the day I was born that love is forbidden to a shaman. So it has always been.

"And neither was my brother the cause of it," White Swan goes on, "no, it is a custom among some of the tribes that the shaman is forbidden to love. But it is only a custom, nothing more, just as men of the west wear their hair long and braided, and those of the eastern tribes do not. Love only makes our souls grow, Asena. I love a man very deeply, and yet my powers are intact.

"Asena, your wolf-guide stopped coming because you would not heed his warnings: you put yourself and others in danger by not telling your kinsmen about my brother. But even had you not lied, do you really think they would have been able to stop Swiftarrow? He is Shaolin. You are not to be blamed for Swiftarrow's deeds. No, it is rage and bitterness that nearly killed your wolf-guide, Asena. It is rage and bitterness that have eaten away the rest of your powers. That is why you do not see my spirit-horse."

"No," I say. I can't breathe. I can't bear it. "Leave me alone."

I run.

In the alley, I crouch in the shadow of the wall, breathing so hard the gate-guards can most likely hear. I do not care. I wrap my arms around my knees, shoulders heaving. The tears chill my face as they fall. I am so cold, but it does not matter. Was the massacre at Claw Rock really not my fault after all? *Could I not have stopped it?* The rush of relief is checked by remembering what I have lost: my powers, my great gift – and my kin. I close my eyes and see that little boy with an arrow in his back, dead. My whole body aches with sorrow. I want to sleep; I must lie down, even if it be here in this rain-puddled street. I do not care.

I am back on the shore of the Summer Lake. Shaman Tulan is waiting for me, sitting beneath his favourite mulberry tree as he gazes out across the waters to the white-shouldered mountains on the far side of our valley. A fire smoulders at his feet. Grey smoke drifts with the wind. I walk towards him, sick with shame, for I must tell Tulan what I have done, that I have allowed myself to be eaten up by hate and rage. He will be so sorry.

As I get nearer, he looks at me, but Tulan does not smile or speak. His eyes do seem to burn me. The wind gets up, stirring his long grey hair, rippling the water's skin, rustling through the mulberry leaves. I sit down beside my old master, and Tulan reaches into the leather bag at his belt and takes out the herb pouch. Wordless, he holds a spray of thyme in the flames till the dried-out leaves glow crackling red and the smell burns my throat. Here's the tug in my belly; I'm leaving my body behind once more.

"Come," says Shaman Tulan. "We must go travelling."

We walk side by side through a silent forest, my old master and I. Sunlight slants down between the larches. Starflower vines hang from the branches of silver-trunked birch trees. The trees thin out and we come to a clearing. A dark shape lies in the middle.

"Go," says Shaman Tulan. "See what you have done."

I walk closer. The dark shape is a dead wolf, a thin, starved creature. The poor beast has died alone. Tears burn my cheeks as I kneel beside him. I reach out and as I lay my hand on the wiry fur, I feel the pulse of life beneath, very faint, but beating all the same.

"What shall I do now?" I turn to Shaman Tulan but he is walking away through the forest. As I watch my master go, he seems to stoop less and move with greater ease, so that now that he is nearly hidden by sunlit trees, he looks like a much younger man, loping along without a care.

I will never see him again.

I lie down beside the wolf and I weep.

A voice comes out of the darkness: "Wake! What fool's game is this, lying in the street like a drunk?"

It is only Swiftarrow. He grips my shoulders, crouching at my side, eyes fixed on mine. Night has fallen. I ache with cold.

"Where have you been?" he hisses. "My sister said you left her hours since. She said you needed to make a journey. What in the name of Heaven has happened?" He pauses, staring. "Why do you look at me so?"

I cannot tell him I am trying to see his spirit-horse. I wait for the silvery flicker of a tossing mane, just a glimpse. But there is still nothing. Swiftarrow reaches out and takes my hand.

"You are so cold." He draws me close and joy floods through me, a line of brightness through misery. At last, at last. We hold each other, Swiftarrow and I. It feels as if we have always done so.

"What is wrong?" he asks, his breath warm against my neck. His hair tickles my face.

How to say it? "It is nothing," I tell him. "Just something that I lost."

"Do not cry," Swiftarrow whispers, the anger quite gone from his voice. "Don't cry, Asena." His hair smells of woodsmoke. He grips my hand in both of his and holds it to his lips, breathing the heat of his body into mine. Swiftarrow. I have been given the gift I ached after for so long, but another is taken from me, gone for ever. I was a shaman. I was born with an extra soul. Now I am nothing. Even if White Swan speaks the truth, and the deaths at the Gathering were not my fault, I cannot bear this. Getting to my feet, I run, leaving Swiftarrow to follow me. He won't catch me this time. Autumn Moon has taught me too well.

For once, I outwit him.

29

Swiftarrow
A short while later

S wiftarrow waited outside the great chamber, listening to music and voices within. The door opened and the servant Jin came out, holding a wine-jug. He bowed.

"You are very late, young master. I understand that Lord Fang most particularly wished you to attend this gathering."

Swiftarrow did not bother to reply, but just walked past him into the chamber, past the throng of purple-robed courtiers seated at the table with their concubines, and knelt before his father.

"Lord Fang, the wayward child appears," someone called out, braying with laughter that echoed around the chamber. Lamps flickered, casting shadows across painted faces; golden light puddled on the floor.

She had not returned to the Forbidden Garden. Where was she? Autumn Moon did not know. At last he had held

Asena in his arms, and now she was gone, fled into the streets. Was she seeking only comfort when I held her? What tormented her? Fear? Was it the loss of her kinsmen, an old wound burst open by being among the Tribes again?

"Where in the Realm of Freezing Hell have you been, Fang Shiyu?" Lord Fang spoke with his usual languor, but Swiftarrow did not miss the iron edge to his voice. "Come, sit by me. Take a drink. No one at your temple shall find out."

Swiftarrow took his place on the couch and as Lord Fang had spoken very quietly into his ear, so low that no one else could hear above the drunken clamour, he realized that his father was as clear-headed as an abbot. How often had Lord Fang appeared drunk when in fact he was not?

"I do not wish to explain this again: you must at least seem a dutiful son of this house, even if you are not," Lord Fang said. "Now tell me, where have you been?"

Sometimes the best lie is closest to the truth. Swiftarrow took the cup of wine from his father's hands. "O lord," he said, "I'm in love with a girl, that's all, but she won't see me. I am sore wounded by love and I did not hear the eighth bell, nor the ninth or tenth. I humbly beg your forgiveness."

He raised the porcelain cup to his lips and drank, hot wine searing down his throat, burning his eyes.

Lord Fang laughed. "You are forgiven, but only if she is the proper kind of wench. I learned too late the dangers of beautiful barbarian girls."

More laughter rippled around the chamber, and Swift-arrow said, "My father is too kind."

Swiftarrow knew he had been given a warning; yet it came too late.

When Lord Fang spoke next, so quietly no one else could hear, the laughter was gone from his voice. "My son, it is time for you and me to make a move in the game."

Swiftarrow drew in a long breath. "O Father, I am ready to play."

30

Asena
Later that night

The courtyard is quiet and the stars are out, the moon a cold white ball hanging in the sky. Is everyone sleeping? I pause, listening, eyes shut. No: I hear four people breathing deep and slow, one faster. There is someone awake. Autumn Moon comes walking out of the dark hall.

"Swiftarrow was afraid for your safety," she tells me. "He came here and said you ran from him, greatly troubled, that you insisted on being alone. Asena, you must both take care. Such violent passions will only lead to pain. I should have forbidden him from bringing a girl his own age to join us." She sighs. "But then we would not have you, so in truth I am glad he did."

I shrug and look at the ground. I sense her watching me.

After a few moments have passed, Autumn Moon speaks again: "What is wrong, Asena? Is it your task for the

Empress? With each day, I expect Brother Snake-eye to return with word from the Abbot. Surely he will be here soon, and then I pray we shall be released from her spider's web. Meanwhile, we must all have patience."

I shake my head, unable to form the words. Tears fall, burning my face. How can I explain to Autumn Moon what I have lost?

"Asena, it will be all right." She steps towards me, holding out her arms, patting my back with clumsy kindness.

How will anything be all right? As if losing my family and home were not enough, now I have lost my wolf-guide for ever, too. I will surely die when I kill the Empress, and I must ride to the World Below without him on a spirit-horse crippled by rage and revenge. I must leave Swift-arrow behind. I don't want to.

"Help me," I beg her. "Please."

Autumn Moon releases me, stepping back a few paces. "Come," she says. "I will be your pain, and you shall battle it." She bows her head and I bow, too, taking a long breath. I must be calm. I must be ready. Without any other warning, Autumn Moon pounces at me faster than a scorpion's tail rising to sting. I run like a monkey up the wall, but she is here to meet me. Our hands meet and we push away, grabbing each other, twisting, releasing; wolf, dragon, swallow.

The red light of dawn spills across the courtyard, setting fire to the bronze bowl resting on the shrine. Autumn Moon and I have been sparring all night. Hours have slipped into nothing – gone as we travelled the Way together. The steady beat of Hano chopping mushrooms and onions for broth drifts from the cook-room.

Autumn Moon steps away, bowing once more. She smiles at me, her thin, bald-headed face bright with the joy of true peace. She reminds me of a baby bird fallen from the nest, but she has the strength of an eagle. "Come," she says, "the rest of them shall be ready for fast-break by now. Let us join them. We must eat, after all."

I bow back, hoping she cannot see my true thoughts. Yes, I too found peace this night, but nothing else has changed. If I do not kill the Empress of the T'ang, the Horse Tribes will never be safe. I have given up my wolf-guide as lost; I know my spirit is broken.

It does not matter. *I* do not matter. Soon I will be gone from this world, but my people will ride free under the great, stretching skies of the steppe for ever.

31

Asena
One night later

I crouch outside the firelit tent, hands clenched into fists, trying to keep my fingers warm. Spit pools in my mouth at the smell of cooked meat drifting from the smoke-hole. Smoke rises, too, thick and pale against the darkness. Flakes of ash hang on the air like the petals of a flower: it is a windless night. I hear someone moving about within, a woman's voice, the cry of a child.

I wish Swiftarrow were here at my side but then he would see how afraid I am, and I could not bear the shame. Even though I have chosen to kill the Empress, chosen to die, the truth of it keeps creeping up behind me me: I love him.

This is the right place: I have watched it long enough to see who comes in and who goes out, but the one I seek is not here yet. Because the tent is lit from within, I am able see the woman moving about inside, just a shadow. She bends low, picking something up, then straightens. I hear a thin cry and soft soothing words. The woman is holding a child. Her shadow wobbles, grows smaller. She has gone. In my mind, I see her walking swiftly through the camp with the child bundled in deerskin and rugs.

I still cannot see their spirit-horses. My wolf-guide shall never run at my side again. I have chosen my path.

Most likely this girl shall join a fireside gathering of women all drinking kumis and cooing over the brats till the small ones fall asleep. But enough of this – dreaming of home will make me weak.

I must get inside before Lord Ishbal returns. These outer skins are pegged down hard, but this shall not be the first time I have sneaked into a tent. Shemi and I used to do so all the time. This is a large one, with many stuffed cushions and rich furs lining the walls. In the middle, a fire burns in an iron bowl, sending coils of smoke up around the poplar-trunk pole that holds the tent upright. Beside the fire, covered bowls are laid out on a red and white striped rug. Real food: cooked meat, yogurt, cheese and good thick milk. Tea with hot salty butter. I crouch behind the pile of skins, aching to fill my belly. This night, Hano served noodle broth and fried pickled cabbage. Ah, what I would not do for a mouthful of fire-charred meat and some salty tea—

But wait, I hear footfalls growing slowly louder – a man walking with the lopsided bow-legged saddle gait of the Horse Tribes. I watch as the tent-flap falls open, and a man stoops on his way in, followed by a blast of cold air. He straightens up, letting the flap fall back behind him, shutting out the night. It is Lord Ishbal. I recognize his hollow-cheeked face, dark with half-grown beard. If I did not already know his right hand was missing, I don't think I would have spotted the lack of it straight away – he moves with swift grace, shrugging off his cloak and slinging it across a low wooden stool. If only I could see his spirit-horse I would know what manner of man he is, twisted with wickedness or longing to change for the better.

Lord Ishbal sits down on the men's side of the fire, picking up a steaming cup. He blows gently then drains it in one gulp. Hot tea. Now he lifts the covers from the bowls and picks up a skewer of meat, dipping it into the yogurt. *Oh, stop.* I can't bear to watch. Ishbal chews slowly, gazing into the fire.

I must do this. Taking a long breath, I stand up, showing myself.

Slowly, Lord Ishbal turns to face me. For a moment, we stare at one another. I may be dizzy with terror but I won't show it.

At last, the one-handed man smiles. "So you are the one White Swan sent. Come, sit. I have never seen a child with such hunger in her eyes."

Is he trying to throw me off guard with a show of kindness, this man who calls himself Son of the Sky Father?

Slowly, I walk towards him, one foot at a time. There's a knife in my belt but I don't want him to know it. Ishbal just waits, warming himself by the fire as if he hasn't a care. I crouch down beside him, sitting cross-legged. Lord

Ishbal says nothing, just hands me the bowl of meat. It's deer, lumps of deer-meat on skewers, fire-charred and juicy. I eat in silence and, *oh*, it is good. The flesh is crunchy and blackened on the outside, but still bloody within. He gives me yogurt, too, salty and cool, and pours tea from a silver-wrought pot, spooning a knob of butter in so that yellow suns of fat float on top, and he does it all with just one hand. The buttery tea runs down my throat, warming my belly. At last I'm full and I wipe the grease from my face.

"I thank you," I whisper.

Ishbal shrugs, gazing into the fire. "In payment, tell me why you seek an audience with me. I have never seen your face before. You are not a daughter of this camp, yet you are of the Tribes. Did you escape from the slave-market in Chang'an? I have spent more than your weight in gold free-ing tribesfolk from that place."

Is that true? In my mind, I had woven Lord Ishbal in the same pattern as my uncle Taspar: brash, loud and foolish. But he is nothing like that. He is not what I expected at all.

I swallow the last of my tea and turn to meet his eyes. I came here to speak with this man, and so I shall: "No. Do you know of the Shaolin?"

Lord Ishbal spits into the fire. "Holy men who spy for the Empress these days, or so I'm told. And what have the holy men to do with a ragged Horse Tribe girl sneaking around my camp?"

"I am one of them, my lord." How quick can I reach my knife if I need it? Ishbal wears a leather-sheathed dagger at his belt. The words rush from my lips: "The truth of it is the Empress suspects you are no longer loyal to her: she sent me here to listen in on all your talk. Are you loyal to her, my lord?"

Lord Ishbal watches the fire, saying nothing. A curl of dry bark catches light and burns to ash, floating up towards the smoke-let.

My heart hammers but I know this trick: he keeps quiet so that I talk. But I have said enough.

At last, Ishbal speaks, still gazing at the flames. "But you no longer wish to do the Empress's bidding, do you, girl? Where do your kin ride?"

"Away to the west, many moons' ride beyond the desert – those who weren't killed by the Empress's men at the Gathering." I spit out the words. But I am meant to be asking the questions, not he. "Is it not time you led your people away from the shadow of Chang'an and rode with the Tribes, not against them?" I draw in a deep breath. "Do you not long to ride free again, my lord?"

Ishbal glances at me, sharply. "White Swan told you this?" He shakes his head. "Ah, well, a man may only feast on what he hunts. I am her uncle, and my father played the girl an ill turn when he left her and her mother in that whorehouse: now she moves against me. What became of the other child? A boy, wasn't it?"

I flinch. I'm not about to tell Ishbal anything about Swiftarrow.

"So," Lord Ishbal says, "your kin were killed and you were

taken by the Empress's men. This is your revenge. Foolish of the Empress to have chosen you out of all the Shaolin to spy on the Tribes."

"Such is her arrogance, she believes one so lowly as I would never dare disobey her."

Ishbal nods, slowly, and I see the glimmer of a smile. "Her mistake." The smile fades as quick as it came, and his eyes do seem to burn into me. "But you ought to take care, girl. You play a dangerous game."

"I am honour-bound to finish it. My people went to the World Below with no death-rites. Their bones whiten at the foot of Claw Rock, unburied; their souls surely wander."

He sighs. "Heavy is my duty this night. I cannot see where my loyalty should lie, child. My people are safe here in the shadow of Chang'an; yet in our hearts we long for the open grasslands. If we ride away with the Empress's army and leave them, seeking our own freedom, they will hunt us down."

"We are all Horse Tribes; we ride fast, and the grasslands are wide, with so many forests and mountains. The Empress's men are wall-dwellers. They won't find you."

Lord Ishbal meets my eyes. "Yet you say your kin were killed by T'ang soldiers at the Gathering."

"We were taken by surprise. Slaughtered – children, too." And again I wonder, *Can Swiftarrow truly be trusted?* "My lord, if the Tribes ride together, the T'ang army has not the smallest chance of catching us. Send envoys to the half-breeds who ride with the Empress's men. Offer them gold and they shall join you. Their loyalty lies with the highest bidder."

Lord Ishbal nods, slowly. He stares into the fire. "I admire your courage, for it is greater than mine. I am ashamed. I shall turn my mind to what you have said. Now go, and make sure you tell the Empress I am loyal only to her. Now we are all playing your dangerous game, girl."

I should be afraid but I'm not: the thrill of revenge is bearing me up on wide, strong wings, higher and higher. Closer to the sun.

32

Swiftarrow
Within the Daming Palace, two hours later

The orchard was cold, the ground hidden by a layer of grey dawn mist. His father had chosen to act, to make a move in the game. Where would this end? Fretting about it would not help: Swiftarrow emptied his mind, becoming one with the trees, one with the mist. Leaving the world of men behind – the sound of many footsteps and soft voices – he travelled the Way, soaring across wastelands of time and space. All was one. Time was as nothing. And then they came, those he had been waiting for: Lord Fang, ghostlike in robes of white, and another man. One-handed and lean as a cat, he walked with the swagger of the Tribes, more used to the saddle: Lord Ishbal. Wrapped in heavy winter cloaks beaded with ant-sized raindrops, Lord Fang and Lord Ishbal waited beneath the bare-branched peach trees. It was raining. Swiftarrow wore no cloak, and his clothes were wet, stuck to his skin. His hair sent little rivers of rainwater down his face. It was time to move.

"My dear son." Lord Fang smiled, mocking as ever, as Swiftarrow stepped out of the mist.

Lord Ishbal flinched. "Cursed Shaolin! You move quicker than rats."

Lord Fang laughed. "He may be Shaolin, but if you do not like it, share the fault with me. I may be the boy's father, but I sired him on your sister. He was there for the taking, had you wanted him."

Lord Ishbal bowed, mocking. "I acknowledge the fault."

Swiftarrow bowed in return. "My lord, we seek only to learn if you are ready to ride out in battle. The great strength of your tribe is sorely needed."

"The Empress waits for your word, Ishbal," Lord Fang said. "General Li has assembled his troops once more. Will you ride with them?"

Lord Ishbal stared back at him, unsmiling. "That's Her Highness's choice. When the coin is sent, we will ride. She may be sure that we shall earn it. My men thirst to avenge themselves on our traitorous brethren across the desert."

"Your wages are being counted and weighed," Lord Fang replied. "I can assure you the matter has the Chief Moneyer's most deep attention. His assistant sent word to me yesterday evening: by sunset tomorrow, you shall have your payment."

Lord Ishbal made another low, mocking bow. "Then at dawn the day after, Lord Fang, my tribe will ride out with General Li and his men." He turned and walked away through the mist, cloak streaming out behind him.

When he was gone, Lord Fang turned to Swiftarrow. "I can only pray this will be enough to shield the House of Fang from the Empress's suspicions: I will make sure she learns it was I who ensured Ishbal's loyalty. These barbarians are always the same: loyal to nothing but gold. And now, tell me – what of the girl?"

"I have her in the palm of my hand: she will do no harm. She knows nothing of our meeting, but believes she has a chance of persuading Lord Ishbal to switch allegiance to the Tribes. Of course, she is wrong."

His father smiled. "Betraying a lover. How exquisitely painful for you. Know this, Fang Shiyu: I will take no pleasure in having the girl killed if you choose to act against me, but I will do it if I must."

Swiftarrow bowed, but when he spoke his voice was hard and cold. "And if you harm her, my lord, I will kill you with my own hands."

"A true Fang warrior after all," his father said, trailing his forefinger down the side of Swiftarrow's face. "The fire burns high with you, does it not? Think of all we could have done together, had fortune decreed otherwise. It is such a dreadful pity. Do you not think so?"

"I am sure you did only what was right, O Father, when you left my sister in the House of Golden Butterflies and me in the temple."

For what seemed a long while, they stood and looked at one another, father and son.

"I am glad you think so." Lord Fang spoke quietly, as if to himself, and indeed Swiftarrow had already gone, lost in the mist among the twisted, naked branches of the peach trees.

33

Asena
East Market, later that day

The sun is sinking above the skyline of Chang'an, spreading fire across the darkening sky. Eighth Daughter tugs at my hand and turns to look at me pleadingly. "Quickly, Asena, or we shan't have time to see the acrobats!" Her cheeks are flushed and red like her tunic – an old, patched one that belonged to Autumn Moon when she was a child.

Can I see it: the faintest, shadowy flicker of a spirit-horse at her right shoulder? Surely this is only my longing to be a shaman again. Eighth Daughter may have had a Horse Tribe slave as her nurse before she came to the temple, but she was born a wall-dweller. Do wall-dwellers really have no spirit-horses? Could it be that the T'ang are no different to the Tribes, and it is only a matter of seeing what one wishes to believe?

"Be calm – I am coming." I struggle to keep the fear from my voice.

I have not seen Swiftarrow since I left him outside the House of Golden Butterflies. He must know I have been to Lord Ishbal by now. So where is he? Does he not care what Ishbal told me? In my mind, I hear Autumn Moon telling me to breathe deeply, to push away all thought. *The Way is open to all, Asena, but you must turn from fear, worry, love, hatred. Everything.*

"We must get the onions first," I hear myself saying. "Hano won't be pleased if they're all sold when we come."

Eighth Daughter tosses her head like a young foal, skinny black pigtails flying. "Hano and his onions, I curse them four times!" she cries, skipping along. "I want nut pastries instead."

I force a laugh. "Maybe if we buy one for Hano too, he'll forgive us spending his coin on pastries."

Where are you, Swiftarrow?

Which path has Ishbal chosen? Will he ride out with the Empress's men? My people are born hunters, trailing deer through dark forests, shooting arrows at fat ducks on the lakeshore, but now they are the hunted. Should I go to White Swan? Perhaps Ishbal has returned to the House of Golden Butterflies; he might have spilled out the secrets of his heart to White Swan again.

I dread seeing her. She will know the path I have chosen, the choice I have made. But my mind is firm: I will kill the Empress.

I turn, glancing over my shoulder. *Is someone watching me?* I see nothing but a gang of children jumping in a puddle longer than two men lying head to feet and the crowd of folk surging about the marketplace, shoving, laughing, crying out their wares. I shudder. It is like that evening in Samarkand, long ago, when Swiftarrow chased me to the gate in the west wall. Only now there is no Baba waiting. I will never see Baba again.

Eighth Daughter skips ahead and leaps right across the puddle, landing neat as a cat on the other side. The other children stop their splashing and stare, astonished: unlike Eighth Daughter, they have not been trained to jump by a taskmaster like Autumn Moon. I grab Eighth Daughter's sleeve and hurry her on: we need not attract the stares of the whole marketplace.

"You go and watch the acrobats – I'll fetch Hano's onions and we'll meet by the willow tree."

She tugs thoughtfully on one pigtail, weighing up the bargain. "But shall we still have pastries?"

"Yes. Now go!"

Eighth Daughter runs into the crowd, pigtails flapping out behind her.

I sense it once more: someone is watching me. I turn. A crowd has gathered by the fortune-teller next to the pastry-stall. Fall-of-leaf sun shafts down through shifting cloud and I see a shadow where there is no one to cast it. Swiftarrow. We run to each other. We stand in the marketplace, his arms around me, mine around him. He is rain-soaked, cold. His hair is wet. Where has he been? I love him; I love him. I crush mistrust like a spider in my hand.

How will I ever explain to him what I have lost: my wolf-guide, my soul?

"Why did you leave me?" he asks. "Where have you been? I was so afraid for you."

"I ask you the same! I went to—"

Swiftarrow shakes his head. "Listen, we have not much time. I saw Lord Ishbal." His breath is warm against my face, his voice calm. "He dares not rebel: his fear of the Empress is too great. With General Li's legion, Ishbal and his people will ride out to hunt down the rest of the Tribes. Your people will be enslaved, broken. Lord Ishbal and the army leave with the coming dawn."

"No!" It can't be true. "He seemed so willing to escape Chang'an. He said… But we agreed that *I* was to go to Ishbal. Why did you go, too?"

Does Swiftarrow not trust me? Or can I really trust him? I push away the thought.

"Ishbal has chosen against us, Asena," Swiftarrow says. "He has accepted the Empress's bribe. Come." He takes my hand, pulling me after him, not giving me the chance to speak. We run through the marketplace, dodging stalls and the shifting crowd till we reach the tree-lined road. It's jammed with jackasses, carts and people shouting at one another to clear the way, as ever, but this day the throng is even thicker. A covered cart is moving slowly through the jumble of traffic, heavily guarded by Gold Birds and men in the livery of the palace. "There." Swiftarrow points. "Lord Ishbal's reward."

"I don't believe it."

"Then I will show you." Swiftarrow breaks away, letting go of my hand. He runs straight to the cart, and not one of the guards turns his head to look, not even when Swiftarrow springs up onto the back of the cart. What is he doing? The crowd shifts again and I can no longer see.

"See." He is at my side again, one arm around my shoulders. He holds up a glittering rope of newly minted ring-shaped coins, each threaded on to a leather cord like beads on a necklace. "Straight from the Moneyer's hall. The whole hoard will reach Lord Ishbal's hands by nightfall."

"Hide it, for the love of Mother Earth!" I hiss, cold with horror.

It is coming. My death. Hand-in-hand with that of the Empress of the T'ang, the spider who waits in the middle of this web. I wanted to die knowing the Tribes were safe, but there must be a thousand coins on this string alone. How much more money lies piled up in the cart? Lord Ishbal will ride out with the Empress's army, and together, they will sweep my people from the face of the earth.

Swiftarrow drops the string of coins into the lap of a beggar crouching outside a tavern. Her astonished blessing fades away as we run, holding hands once more. At last we stop, back in the bustle of the marketplace, and Swiftarrow wipes a tear from my face with the tip of a finger. "Ah, not you, brave one. Don't weep again. We still have a chance of stopping them. Even if Ishbal has chosen the path of cowardice, we know there are men in his camp ready to rebel, and most likely women, too. It is only that we have scarcely any time to rouse them for a fight." He frowns. "What is wrong?"

"Tell me," I say, "why did you go to Ishbal, when we agreed that I would be the one to do it."

"I didn't want you to go," he replies, quickly. "If something were to happen— I am falling in love with you, Asena."

Joy floods through me. It is so cruel that I should know this only to leave it behind. I never thought I should have it at all. I thought I should always be alone. And all along, I could have loved Swiftarrow and been a shaman, too. My people were wrong. Shaman Tulan was wrong. *Love only makes our souls grow, Asena*, White Swan told me. Now I will neither be loved nor a shaman. I will not live to be a mother, bear his children. Swiftarrow and I hold each other so close I feel the beating of his heart; we are one, standing in the rain in the marketplace.

"I love you," he whispers, and I lean against his chest. I do not want him to see these tears. I am leaving him today, for ever. I am going to kill the Empress, and afterwards, I will be killed.

I am the first to break away. "What shall we do?" This is the last time I will see him. I try to fix his face in my mind, the slanting green eyes, the rare smile, so that I shall take the shadow of his beauty with me to the World Below, and his bravery, too.

As if he knows, as if it is goodbye for him, too, Swiftarrow leans closer and kisses me once on the mouth. He smiles, his last gift to me. "We must separate. Two apart can do more than two together."

That is what Baba told me the night of the ambush and I never saw him again. Oh, Baba, I am sorry that you will never find me.

"Return to the Forbidden Garden," Swiftarrow goes on. "I will go straight to the camp and spread word as fast as I can among those who are ready to rebel. They must all ride away from here by dawn." He kisses me again.

I turn and run. I cannot bear to look back and see him for the last time.

Eighth Daughter runs up to me as I sprint into the courtyard. "Where did you go? I waited and waited after the acrobats had finished and you never came!" She looks me up and down. "And you didn't get the onions, either – Hano will—"

"Never mind Hano." I glance around the yard. "Where is everyone?"

"In the hall," Eighth Daughter says. "But listen—"

I've no time for listening. In the hall, Autumn Moon, Red Falcon and Hano sit at the feet of the great bronze statue of the Enlightened One, together with a black-clad Shaolin I've never seen before, and a woman in white commoner's robes. She turns, and I hide my shock: it is White Swan. She has left the House of Golden Butterflies – *she has escaped*. My heart pounds. *What is happening?*

She looks up, eyes resting on me. I feel the heat of her gaze. Her eyes are dark with sorrow as she looks away.

Autumn Moon smiles, calm as ever. "Asena," she says, "come, sit with us. There is much to talk of."

I bow before speaking: "Autumn Moon, Lord Ishbal has accepted the Empress's bribe. He will ride out at dawn: they are going to hunt down the Tribes. We must stop them. Swiftarrow has gone to the camp to see if he can persuade Ishbal's men not to follow him, to rebel."

White Swan draws in a sharp breath. Red Falcon turns his head, very slightly, to look at her. Their eyes meet.

What goes between the two of them? It is as if they spoke without making a sound.

"It shall be Swiftarrow's last task in Chang'an," Autumn Moon says. "Our time here has come to an end. Brother Snake-eye has returned from Mount Shaoshi with the holy Abbot's permission for us to leave." She lays a hand on the stranger's shoulder, who nods – a slim, serious-faced man. "Asena," Autumn Moon goes on, "I must beg you and Swift-arrow to come with us. There is no longer any need to stay in Chang'an. For your own sake, come with us and leave this behind."

But even as Autumn Moon speaks, her eyes are filled with sorrow: she is no fool, and she knows what I am going to say.

"I cannot." Tears slip unbidden down my face. "I must try to save the Tribes. It is my duty."

Autumn Moon smiles at me, and I know I will never see her again once I leave the Forbidden Garden. "Your courage is deep, Asena. At dawn, Red Falcon shall be waiting by the guard-house on the south road, beyond the city walls. He will wait till the sun is just above the horizon."

"Asena?" says White Swan, sharply. "Will you be there?"

"Make sure you send word to Swiftarrow," I reply, trying to keep my voice steady. "I don't know if I will see him again tonight. There will be many people in Ishbal's camp, and it would be easy to miss him."

But I am not going to Lord Ishbal's camp to join forces with Swiftarrow.

He will meet Red Falcon at the rising of the sun. I will not. I am going to the palace.

34

Asena
The Daming Palace

I have come to the heart of the spider's web.

I lie face-down on the beam, looking at the dark chamber below – without Swiftarrow this time. In the middle of the floor sits a high, curtained bed draped with heavy silks. The shutters have been left slightly open and a screen arranged before the window, so that the fall-of-leaf breeze shall not disturb the sleeper when she comes. The faint, earthy scent of cinnabar-paste drifts up to me. The knife strapped to my leg digs into my flesh. What is the quickest way to kill with a knife? I must hammer it straight into her heart. Cutting her throat will take too long, although I would like the Empress of the T'ang to drown in her own blood.

To save my people, I must kill her. There is no choice, and I thirst to do it.

But not yet, not yet. I must wait. Darkness deepens and

my limbs stiffen, burning with the strain of keeping so still. The silken drapes hanging about the Empress's bed billow as a stronger breeze blows past the screen, chilling my skin.

When I slid away from the Forbidden Garden they were rolling up spare clothes, gathering weapons: taking only what could be carried. On foot, the Shaolin will go from Chang'an like swallows flying south for the winter, leaving the temple of the Forbidden Garden empty as a nutshell. The fallen leaves of autumn shall blow across the courtyard with no one to watch them.

Where is Swiftarrow now? Has Autumn Moon sent him the order to leave Chang'an? Is he already in the camp?

Wait. What is that sound? I listen. The song of the palace swells by a hair's breadth: distant voices, the soft thud of an ink-pot laid down on a wooden table, footfalls growing louder. Someone is coming. The door opens, throwing a pool of butter-yellow light across the floor. An old woman shuffles across the chamber holding a lamp, slow with age. She stops and sighs, lays down her lamp on the table beside the bed and turns back the coverings, smoothing them carefully. She turns and shuffles out, closing the door behind her. It shuts with a click.

The Empress is coming to her deathbed.

The lamplight flickers, throwing shadows across the walls. The fire-snakes painted on the screen seem to shiver and uncoil of their own will.

I hear footfalls again. Three sets. Three people. Louder, louder. They are here. The door swings open once more. It is her: the Empress, wrapped in stiff court robes, hair piled high, stuck with peacock feathers, studded with pearls. She is flanked on either side by plain-faced maidservants. So it is true, the old rumour that the Empress will have no fair-faced women within sight. Without a word, the maidservants begin to undress her, untying the robe, lifting it away from her pale, maggoty body. The smell of stale wine billows from her clothes. The last feast of the Chrysanthemum Festival is done with, and soon winter will come. I turn away, letting fresh air drift across my face. When I turn back, the Empress is clad in a night-robe, fluttering blue silk stitched with clouds of butterflies. She sits straight-backed on a stool, and silently the maidservants work at her hair, pulling out pins and combs, unravelling pearls, setting the hair free from its coils.

At last, the maidservants bow low. Will they go now? No. They help the Empress into bed, drawing up the covers, letting the silken drapes fall about the bed, then kneel and take out a pair of sleeping mats from the chest next to the window. Without a word, the maidservants unfold padded quilts, one blows out the lamp, and they lie down side by side at the foot of the Empress's bed like a pair of Eighth Daughter's wooden dolls, ready to do her bidding at any moment.

I wait in darkness, clutching the beam. One after the other, all three women drift into slumber, the Empress and her maidservants, equal in sleep. All helpless.

Things are never as they seem.

What did Swiftarrow mean when he said that? Fear floods through me, sickening. *Where is he now?* The same questions return. Why did Swiftarrow go to Ishbal when we'd agreed the task was mine? If it was to stop me going, why did he not tell me about it sooner?

What if Swiftarrow is not what I think he is?

Did he really go to the camp, begging Ishbal's men to rebel? *What if he did not?*

Has Swiftarrow always been a traitor, and I just a fool? Did he ever really change? If I were still truly a shaman, I would know by looking at his spirit-horse.

I am shaman, as you once were, White Swan had said to me. The great power in you is broken and twisted.

What have I done? I must go to the camp myself. I must warn everyone there to ride hard away from Chang'an before General Li's men are ready to leave, and I must go now. But if I do not kill this spider first, she will live to spin another web.

I draw in one long breath, releasing it slowly. I close my eyes, hearing the voice of Autumn Moon in my mind:

Our sister the swallow thinks nothing of the earth: her place is the sky. Make it yours. Believe this, and so it shall be.

I am a swallow with a forked tail and black wings; I swoop in the warm air, the sun on my back. Leaping, I fly and my heart soars with the thrill of it.

I am Shaolin.

I land in a crouch, silent. *Good.* Autumn Moon would be proud of me. I wait, still. One of the maidservants sighs in her sleep, turns. Her breathing slows again. Three heartbeats pound along with my own, the last music I shall ever hear.

I am coming, O Imperial Majesty. I am coming for you.

All is quiet.

A breeze slides in through the window, past the screen. Silk drapes billow about the Imperial bed. Rising, I slide free the knife from the scabbard strapped to my calf. The blade shines, moonlit. I run to the bed. The Empress lies on her back, mouth slightly open, breathing heavily. Her face is pale. Her eyebrows are faint, sea-green paint wiped away till tomorrow – but tomorrow will never come. Not for her. Her lips are slack.

Goodbye, O Majesty.

I lift the knife— What is that? Another heartbeat: a fourth heartbeat. There is someone behind me. *Shaolin.* I whirl around to face them.

It is Swiftarrow. He grabs my arm, squeezing my wrist.

"Drop the knife," he hisses.

I should never have trusted him.

On the bed beside us, the Empress opens her eyes. She screams, sitting up, clutching the covers to her chest. Swiftarrow knocks the knife from my hand. The maidservants are screaming, too. I hear the pounding rhythm of heavy men running, their feet hammering the floor; I hear their ragged breathing. I stand still, staring at Swiftarrow. Once an enemy, always an enemy. How foolish I was to think it would be any different.

"Give me the knife," I say, calm as if I were speaking of a

cook-room spoon. "I will finish this." He has betrayed me again. He did not truly love me. Most likely all that was a trick. All just a trick.

"No!" begs the Empress. "You cannot kill me." Her voice rises to a high-pitched whine. "My guards will cut your throat. You are just a young girl. You do not want to die."

Swiftarrow grabs at my arm again but I dodge him, snatching back the knife, moving faster than flame-hot mercury. The guards come closer, closer, their footfalls louder and louder.

Swiftarrow lunges forward; he's trying to get the blade, but I slide away faster than a snake. I laugh. "The door is locked. And I am no fool, O Imperial Highness. If I let you live, you will most likely have me thrown down a well."

"No," wheedles the Empress, "I should never do that to a brave girl such as you." Her tone changes, becomes confiding. "We live in a world ruled by men, little Shaolin maiden. Strong women should stand by one another."

"Do not do it, Asena," Swiftarrow says. "Don't become a killer. Not for her."

I turn to him. *What?* Once again, the world around us fades to nothing, as it did the first time we met in the streets of Samarkand. It is just Swiftarrow and I.

"I did not come here to betray you." He leaps forwards, snatching the knife, hurling it past the terrified, shivering maidservants to a far corner of the chamber where it slams point-first into the wall and sticks there, hilt quivering.

"Run," Swiftarrow hisses at me. "Run!"

35

Swiftarrow

I t was too late. The door burst open, splintering off the hinges, and the chamber was filled with guards. There were too many of them to fight, Swiftarrow knew it, and Asena stood like a ghost. The Empress and her maid-servants were screaming, pointing at Asena, but he could not make sense of the words. Everything seemed to be moving so slowly, like bubbles drifting through warm honey. The guards rushed at Asena and she fell to the floor, crushed beneath them. Her head bounced against the floor and a dark stain spread, pooling blood. Letting out a harsh cry, Swiftarrow leapt at the guards, but although there were five on Asena, holding her down even though she lay limp as a doll, five more came for him. Hands snatched at his clothes. Blows landed on his body. And all the while, the high, unbearable shrieking wailed on. More people rushed into the chamber, fanning the Empress, holding herbs beneath her nose to revive her. Pain burst in Swiftarrow's head, throughout his whole body. Desperate, he clawed his way across the floor, trying to reach Asena, but the guards yanked her limp body upright and she was dragged away, head lolling, blood on her neck, face and clothes, dripping from her nose.

"No!" Swiftarrow screamed. "No!" And as darkness claimed him, he thought, *This is how her father felt when I took her.*

He awoke, shivering. It was cold, very cold. Harsh light flooded his eyes. He sat up, holding his aching head. They were outside on dew-damp grass, and dawn had come. His sight cleared and he reached out to touch the bamboo bars of the cage. They were strong, still green, woven close together. Asena lay still in a cage just next to his, the bars almost touching, her blood-stained face grey, sunken. He watched the rise and fall of her chest. She was breathing. She was alive. Dread crushed joy.

But for how long?

They were caged in the Forbidden Garden, dying among the peach trees. Morning had come. Red Falcon had waited for them outside the eastern wall of Chang'an, but now he would be leaving, mounting up, riding to join White Swan and Autumn Moon, Hano, little Eighth Daughter and Snake-eye on the great journey to Mount Shaoshi.

There is no one to help us. They have gone. They know nothing about this, and we are going to die.

At least White Swan was safe, out of the city.

Sickness gripped Swiftarrow's belly. How would Asena and he be punished? How would they die? It would not be quick. Would they both be beaten to death, or strangled beneath the willow tree in the East Market? Strangulation would be a dreadful way to die, worse than beheading, but at least he would return to the ancestors with his body whole. He shuddered, trying to swallow his fear. *That's just a foolish fireside tale. It does not matter what happens to this body, I will be reborn and know nothing of it. It will soon be over,* he thought. *It will soon be done with.*

Or would it? Would they both starve to death here in these bamboo cages, watched by courtiers in silken robes? If they were given no water, it would take only a few days. With water, it would be ten-night after ten-night before death came. He would not allow that. He would rather kill Asena himself than allow her to starve. But how?

Would Lord Fang come? Swiftarrow wished that his were a true father, one who would try to save him if he could. *But even if he were, I have brought shame on the House of Fang. He would be happy to kill me with his own hands for this.* No, there would be no rescue, no way out but to meet death with courage.

Asena stirred, moaning softly, and he laid a hand flat against the bars of his cage, the closest he could get to touching her. Slowly, she sat up. She looked dreadful: dark bruises beneath her eyes, her face blood-smeared; still he loved her.

"Asena," he whispered.

She put a hand against the bars of her own cage, stretching out her fingers to his, but the cages were too far apart. "I am so sorry—" For a moment, her gaze left his face and she seemed to be looking at something over his shoulder.

Fear gripped him again. "What? Do they come now?"

But she only shook her head, smiling. Tears ran down her face, mingling with the dried blood.

"You have a beautiful soul," she whispered. "A strong, beautiful soul."

He did not know what she meant, and so they just sat in silence, separated by bars of green bamboo.

"Do you hear that?" Asena demanded then, pressing her hand palm first against the ground. "Do you feel it?"

Frowning, Swiftarrow laid both hands on the earth, closing his eyes. "They are riding. Lord Ishbal's tribe are riding away."

He would have to tell her. There had been too many lies. "I want you to know the truth," he said: "my father paid Ishbal to go with the Empress's army. And I let him do it. I stood there and I let him do it. He swore he would have you killed if I tried to stop him. I don't expect you to believe that, but it's true."

She did not speak, only looked at him through the green bars of their cages. *Just like in Samarkand,* he thought. *It's as if she can see into my mind.* And he wanted so much to hold her, but he could not.

"I know you are telling the truth," she said, at last. She

smiled. "I know. You did all you could and more. You wouldn't let me become a murderer."

They reached out again, hands pressed against green bars, unable to hold one another. She had forgiven him.

They were going to die, and he would be repaid in the next life for the deaths he had caused. First the Gathering, now Li was chasing after the rest of the Tribes.

Asena had forgiven him.

What will it be, he wondered. *Dog, worm, beggar, hungry ghost, demon?*

And as if she could see what he was thinking, Asena whispered, "Hush."

36

Asena

The light has changed. Shadows grow longer. Night will soon fall. All day long, no one has come. There is no water. Swiftarrow sleeps in his cage, too far away to hold, lying on his back in the grass, his hair very black against the green. I found a handful of small stones, and showed him how to suck them and bring spittle into the mouth as we used to do on the hunt if water was scarce, but we shall not last long without anything to drink. If we are still here when dawn comes, at least we will be able to suck dew from the grass. I do not know if we should.

I do not want to die slowly. I know now that I do not want to die at all. Swiftarrow does not deserve to, and because of me, he shall.

Even if he had not come, and I had killed the Empress, nothing would have changed. Why did I ever think that her death would save my people? If she died a thousand times, the T'ang and the Horse Tribes shall always be neighbours, two empires side by side, one great, one scattered and faded. Nothing I can do will ever change that.

And now we are here, caged among the peach trees in the Forbidden Garden, waiting to die—

I hear people coming: six men, by the sound of their heavy footfalls. Through my misery, I smile. They are taking no chances with us, then. Swiftarrow sits up, shaking off sleep instantly.

"There are too many," he whispers. "Do not try to fight them. We must save our strength – there may be a chance later…"

He does not finish speaking. If we are taken to meet our deaths in the marketplace, there will be no other chance. We shall be surrounded by crowds of people, all eager to watch us die, hungry with the thrill of it. I draw in a long breath and let it go, slowly. I must be the master of this fear.

Swiftarrow turns and smiles at me. "Come," he whispers. "If we are going to die, let us face it so bravely that they are all ashamed."

The crowd's roar is like the cry of a huge wild beast. The roof of the carriage is chained down; iron clinks against wood, and it is so dark in here I cannot even see my own hand. We cling to each other, thrown about like raggedy-dolls as the carriage rolls through the street, growing closer with every moment to the East Market. It stinks in this prison-cart –

a fog of urine, sweat and worse things, all wound about with the sweetish, rotten smell of pure fear.

This cannot be happening, I keep thinking. *They cannot take my life. It is mine.* But it is happening and there is nothing we can do. Autumn Moon, Red Falcon and Hano will be far away by now, journeying east towards Mount Shaoshi. I long to hold on to Swiftarrow but both of us are bound, hands wrenched behind our backs, knotted tight at the wrists. The cart slows to a halt and the roaring of the crowd swells, growing louder and louder.

"Word has spread," Swiftarrow says. "They know we tried to kill the Empress."

"It was not you," I whisper. "It was me. They must let you go. They must."

In the dark, I sense him turning to me. "It is not your fault," he says. "I do not want to walk this earth without you, and I would die for you a hundred times."

Hot tears burn my face.

Chains shriek and clank, harsh light floods the carriage and the guards reach in to drag us out. We land on our knees, hauled to our feet. The noise from the crowd is unbearable – I want to put my hands over my ears, but I cannot. For a moment, I fear my legs are about to give way but I take strength from Swiftarrow; his bruised, bloodied face is calm as he looks out at the mass of people swarming in the marketplace like maggots through a piece of old meat. There's the willow tree. Beneath it, we shall die.

"Come on, no lagging!" the guard shouts, clouting me

about the head. Another roar rises up from the crowd – it's an angry sound, the whine of a wounded beast.

Swiftarrow turns to face me. His guard gives him a clout, too, and the roaring rises up again like the buzzing of a thousand angry wasps. Ignoring the guard, he turns again, giving me a smile that cuts at my heart. "Look," he says, pointing. "We are honoured. She has come to watch us depart."

I follow his eyes down to the willow tree. The Emperor's black hunting carriage waits a few paces away, lacquered all over with birds and beasts. Gold Bird Guards hold back the throng of people, leaving a clearing around the carriage. One of Swiftarrow's guards hits him, harder than before, and I see blood trickling from his lip. The roar swells again till it feels as if the sky must burst.

"Take care, you fool," one of my guards shouts. "This looks to turn bad. Let's just do our work and be gone—"

He is silenced by a rotten onion, flung from deep within the crowd. It bursts against his shoulder.

"They are barely more than children!" someone shouts. "It's not right!"

The guards rush us forwards, cursing. I trip and am dragged along on my knees. They are torn to ribbons and bleeding hard, but it does not matter. Soon it will not matter at all—

He has an axe. The executioner has an axe. I am flooded with relief that we are not to be strangled or beaten to death but the last of Swiftarrow's colour drains from his face.

The Gold Bird Guards hold back the crowd as we are

dragged beneath the willow tree. Trailing branches so green and gold brush my face. The last time I will touch a tree. The Gold Birds are not having an easy time – they lash at the people with sticks, screaming at them to stay back, but still everyone surges forward. Something brushes my forehead and I look up. Dried petals falling, pale against the grey sky. The crowd is throwing handfuls of dried peach petals at us; they float to earth like snow in the mountains. I shall never see snow again; I shall never ride beneath the sky in the light of dawn. Fear must have robbed my wits because a faint, silvery fire flickers above the throng of people and, as I watch, I realize I am looking at a great, wild herd of spirit-horses, bucking, rearing and wheeling about. White Swan was telling the truth after all. The T'ang have spirit-horses. Even the executioner with his axe has a spirit-horse. He is staring at the ground, and so is his spirit-horse, head hanging low.

I see it now: before, I could not see what I did not believe in. I did not believe that the T'ang were just like me. But they are. We are all the same. We are all children of earth. We are born and we shall all die, loving and laughing, hating and weeping together. We are all one.

I hope the executioner kills Swiftarrow first, so he does not have to watch me die.

A lone wolf walks out of the crowd, seen by no one save me. I reach for him. *You have come!*

Yes, because you have opened your heart. You shall not go to the World Below alone, he says, and a grain of comfort swells in my belly.

The door of the black carriage swings open and a sudden, thick hush settles. Two palace guards step out, clad in leather armour. I hear Swiftarrow's heartbeat speeding up. The armoured guards help the Empress out of the carriage. She looks like a bejewelled doll, face powdered white, lips painted blood-red, hair piled up and dotted with bright feathers and pearls. Robes of scarlet flow like bloody water against the black carriage.

My wolf-guide snarls at the sight of her and I wish Swiftarrow could see him, but he is not paying any heed.

"Listen," Swiftarrow hisses, leaning towards me. "Hoofbeats. A rider."

He is right. I hear it, too, just below the great surging cry of the crowd: hoofbeats pounding the earth. A wild blaze of hope burns within me. Can it be Autumn Moon? Did they turn back; did the Shaolin hear somehow that we were prisoners? Maybe White Swan had a dream—

"Let them die!" The Empress's voice rises in a shriek. Her painted, powdered face is screwed up with rage, and I see now that she is mad. Through my fear, I wonder how long ago she lost her wits, and if those fluttering, fondling courtiers know it, too. This whole great, beautiful, rotten empire is ruled by a man too sick to leave his bed and a madwoman. *Once in a thousand years the chance must come for a woman to rule the world,* I think, *and you took it, O Great Empress. When you are gone, men will never allow a woman to gain such power again: you have betrayed us all.* I am shoved to my knees and pain shoots through my legs. Never mind;

never mind. I will feel nothing soon. I clench my hands into fists behind my back, digging my fingernails into my palms. The fear is worse. Now there is a tiny wisp of hope riding towards us on horseback, I do not want to die. Please, please, please let it be Autumn Moon.

The rider is coming closer. Autumn Moon, Red Falcon, is that you? I look up.

It is Lord Fang, clad in ice-white robes that fly out like the wings of a swan as he gallops closer. The crowd scatters around him, pulling each other desperately out of his way. Maybe, just maybe— Yet the last time I saw Lord Fang, he struck Swiftarrow across the face.

So this is it. We are going to die. Autumn Moon is not coming.

But what is he doing here? I turn to Swiftarrow. "Look!" I whisper. *"Look."*

Swiftarrow only shrugs and stares at the ground.

"Get out of my way!" Lord Fang roars, his voice torn to rags. The Gold Bird Guards let him past. Reining in his mare just next to the Empress's carriage, he dismounts. He is not drunk. His spirit-horse stands still, firm at his shoulder, burning with a steady light.

Lord Fang drops to his knees before the Empress, bowing so low that he must be covering those icy robes with filth.

"Rise, Fang." The Empress smiles, as if all this is a jest for her amusement. "What can you want?"

Lord Fang gets to his feet, turning to us, and his face is smeared with mud from the ground. "My son's life," his voice rings out. The crowd is silent. It is as if the whole world has stopped breathing. "I would have my son's life, O Empress of Eternal Light, and that of his beloved."

Still, Swiftarrow does not look up.

The Empress laughs. "But what will you give me instead, Lord Fang? I must have blood. Your son and his beloved committed an act of the highest treason. Who shall pay? Someone must."

"I will," says Lord Fang. "Take my life for both of theirs."

"No!" Swiftarrow's voice is sharp and clear. "Just spare Asena. Spare my father. But take me."

Lord Fang turns, kneeling before him. I look away. "Do not be a fool, my child – you are young and you love one another," he whispers. "It is perfectly beautiful, better than autumn leaves on the surface of a pool, or cherry-blossom blown in the wind." Lord Fang bows to me. "So you see, a bad man can do good. Do not forget that good men can also do wrong. I beg you, take better care of him than I have."

"Very well!" calls the Empress. "I will take you, Lord Fang, in exchange. And greatly I shall miss your poetry, so I am indeed making a sacrifice."

Lord Fang gets to his feet and kneels before her. "Your Majesty. You are so very kind."

The executioner hefts his axe, lifting it high in the air. The blade glitters in the cold light. Rain starts to fall, silvery drops tumbling from the sky.

"No!" Swiftarrow shouts. "No!"

It is too late. The axe has fallen. The crowd roars –

a crashing sweep of sound louder than a snow-slip in the mountains.

The Empress is laughing. "What a foolish man!" she shouts. "Poor Lord Fang. He never saw that life was not poetry – kill the traitors."

The executioner pauses, holding the axe-haft awkwardly in both hands as though he does not know what to do with it, even though Lord Fang's head lies in the mud just paces away.

"Kill them!" the Empress screams, half drowned out by the roaring of the crowd. The Gold Bird Guards are being pushed forwards. They cannot hold back the people.

Swiftarrow is still kneeling, head bowed to the ground, but I struggle to my feet. The guards don't push me back down; they are staring from the executioner to the Empress and back again.

What's that? I see a shadow where there is no one to cast it, just by the Empress's carriage. And another. And another. Now they are gone.

Still, the executioner hesitates, looking from us to the Empress, yet not daring to speak.

"Move!" Autumn Moon hisses. Relief floods through my body from head right down to my feet. She is behind me. Autumn Moon is here. She has come. The rope cuts into my wrists as she tugs, sharply. My hands are free. I turn, time slowing down, to see Red Falcon freeing Swiftarrow, hauling him to his feet, shaking him, shouting into his face, "Run. Run!"

I snatch at Swiftarrow's hand, burning with hot, wild joy. We are free. The guards wheel around, frantic. "Where are they?" shouts one. "Where did they go?"

The executioner drops his axe and runs, lost in the crowd.

"Kill them!" The Empress's voice rises up above the clamour: a ragged, mad shriek. But no one is listening to her.

Think of nothing; think of nothing. We are not here. Do not look at us, there is no use in it—

All around us, the crowd presses in – commoners in dirty white robes, merchants leading asses, grubby-faced children, old men in felt hats, a woman selling pastries from a basket.

We are gone, hidden by Chang'an, drifting away like leaves on the autumn wind; we are safe.

37

Asena

The inn on the post-road is empty, its sloping rooftops shadowed by plane trees. A lone pig noses about in the dusty courtyard. We stop, breathing hard. Swift-arrow takes my hand, still silent.

"Come," Autumn Moon says. "We tethered the horses in woodland, out of sight. We near on have enough mounts for all – Eighth Daughter can ride with me." She points at a straggling stand of bare-branched trees. Rain-filled clouds scud across the sky. It is cold, but I do not care. We are alive. We follow Autumn Moon and Red Falcon to the trees. I see the others already, I sense the dreams of gathered horses, longing for a gallop.

This place is no good as cover. We must get away from here as fast as we can. It shall not be long before the Gold Birds catch up. Every guard in Chang'an will be searching for us by now.

Hano, Snake-eye, White Swan and Eighth Daughter wait beneath a pine tree, huddled together for warmth. The horses stand near by, ears flattened back against their heads – they know we are hunted. Eighth Daughter is the first to run, stirring up a shower of pine needles and dead leaves as she hurls herself at Swiftarrow, then at me.

"We thought you were dead!" she cries. "The lady had a dream!"

White Swan walks slowly towards us but passes Swiftarrow by and takes Red Falcon's hand.

So this is how it shall be. Wordless, they hold one another, the courtesan and the holy man.

Swiftarrow stares, then looks away.

"It's good," I tell him. "Don't you see?"

"It is all right, you know," Eighth Daughter said, tugging at Swiftarrow's tunic. "He has given up his vows. It is allowed."

"Autumn Moon," Snake-eye says. "We must move on. We are hunted."

"We have the start on the Gold Birds – we should use it," Hano adds.

"You are right: they will be following us already." Autumn Moon's face glistens with sweat. Hano passes her a flask and she takes a long draught then wipes her mouth. "We must move. Now is no time to speak of love."

"I will look after her," Red Falcon says to Swiftarrow, quietly. "I swear it."

Swiftarrow nods. Then he turns to his sister, finding his

voice at last. "You were wrong," he says. "Sometimes a cat can be a dog."

What is he talking about? Somehow, White Swan seems to know. Tears spill down her cheeks. She reaches out and takes Swiftarrow's hand. He lifts it to his lips, kissing her.

"We must move," Autumn Moon says again. "Eighth Daughter, come – mount."

Eighth Daughter has started to weep. "Don't go, come with us to Mount Shaoshi! Please come with us."

Swiftarrow lifts Eighth Daughter high in the air and sits her in the saddle before Autumn Moon. "Be brave, little swallow. I have a task. I must take Asena back to her kin. You must swear to look after my sister for me. Do you swear it?"

Eighth Daughter nods, her face streaming with tears.

And now I feel it: the hammering drumbeat of galloping horses. Everyone freezes, save White Swan, who just looks pale with fear.

"They are coming," Autumn Moon says.

There is a flurry of hugging; we clutch each other desperately, whispering our goodbyes. At last, they are all mounted up except Swiftarrow and I, left with the strongest two mares, for we have the furthest to travel. We stand shoulder to shoulder, watching them go. We are left alone.

Swiftarrow turns to me, as if woken from a dream. "What do you wait for?" he says. "Hurry. My father did not give himself up to the axe only for us to be caught by the Gold Birds."

We run; I leap into the saddle and Swiftarrow scrabbles to find his seat – he will get better at that, I hope. I burn with the thrill of being on horseback; I am no hunter but the hunted. We both are.

We turn the horses to the west, and gallop towards the setting of the sun.

Epilogue

Samarkand,
many months later

We walk through the pepper-market, my hand in hers. Dusk is falling. The streets are crowded and the long, heartbreaking song of the Mohammedan call to prayer rings out. We stop at the Hippodrome gates.

"I hope the horse-traders are still taking coin," she says, jingling the leather bag that hangs around her neck.

I can't keep from smiling. Will she never learn? "Do you want every thief in Samarkand on our trail? Hide it, or you shall have to cut open ten more boils and free another old woman of a demon, O great shaman, before we can buy new horses."

"Yes, yes." Impatient, full of fire, she tosses the money bag from one hand to the other. "You chased me along this street. Do you remember? I thought my heart would burst with fear."

"And I was ready to burst with rage when you got away."

We both smile to hide our sorrow.

"I will never find Baba, will I?" Asena says, quietly. "It's hopeless – the Roads are too long and too tangled. Perhaps he gave up looking for me and rode back to camp. It has been nearly a year."

The Hippodrome gates open and a trader pushes past us, letting the gates slam behind him. We step out of his path. Asena watches him go, then freezes like a mouse before a snake. Suddenly, she drops the money bag. Her hands are shaking. I pick it up, squeezing her hand. Do these old memories sadden her too much? Yet I cannot wish that I never found her, never took her. I only wish I had never betrayed the Tribes to that fat old general. I wonder what became of him? Did General Li even bother going back to Chang'an? He'd be better off deserting than trying to explain to Her Majesty that Lord Ishbal just rode off with the Imperial coin and never even fired an arrow. When we caught up with him four days' ride west of Chang'an, he insisted on escorting the pair of us safely across the Great Desert, back to the green grasslands of the steppe.

I don't want her to cling to hope of finding her father when there is none. "Should we ride north and meet with Ishbal?" I say. "Or first search for the rest of your kin? You know Ishbal said we would always be welcome— Asena? What is the matter?"

From across the street, I hear the horse-trader saying, "There's a fine beast. How much do you want for him?"

"He is not for sale."

I know that voice. I have heard it before – from a blood-stained man with a wounded leg, lying helpless on the ground, begging me not to take his daughter.

She is staring across the street, wordless for once.

"The loss is yours, my friend." The horse-trader walks away, off towards the pepper-market.

Here they are, a man leading a horse. He drags one leg slightly as he walks. The horse lifts his head and stops, standing stiller than a rock.

"Come, Shadow, what's amiss?" says the man, patting the horse's neck, running his fingers through the pale mane. Her father. O Lord Fang, does your headless ghost still walk the streets of Chang'an, or were you born into greater peace this time, away from palaces, courtesans and lovers?

"Baba!" Asena calls. "Baba! What is wrong with you? Are you blind?"

What penance will he ask of me? I will do anything but leave her, and he will not ask it, for he loves her too much. I can see that in his disbelieving, delighted smile, even as his gaze falls on me; he knows who I am, what I did – though not all.

I let go of her hand so she can run to him.

Historical Note

*S*pirit Hunter is just a story, but it is rooted in one of the wildest and most fascinating chapters of history ever written. For nearly 3,000 years merchants, monks, artists and fugitives traded, preached and stole along a great tangle of age-old trade routes running through Central Asia between China, Europe, North Africa, India and Persia – known today as the Silk Road. Very few, if any, travellers followed the whole route: there was such a vast muddle of paths with so many different beginnings and endings. A silk merchant in Chang'an, China, for example, would not travel with his cargo all the way to Venice – after stopping at an inn, he would sell his goods to another merchant, and slowly the silk made its way west, passing through the hands of many traders until it reached the marketplaces of Europe. The journey was by no means easy: many travellers died in the icy mountain passes and lonely roadside inns. Many more left behind their bones in the Taklamakan Desert and the sandy wastelands of Lop Nur, led from the safety of their companions by mirages – false images of cool, glittering water and shady trees, just tricks of the mind.

But people did not only endure such hardship to make money. Over a thousand years ago, near a gorge in the Flaming Mountains of western China on the edge of the Taklamakan Desert, seventy-seven caves were cut into the rock. These caves hide enormous paintings, hundreds upon hundreds of years old. Amongst scenes from the life of Buddha and princes and princesses from local tribes there are pictures of blue-eyed Buddhist monks, evidence that a religion born in India had reached the blue-eyed nomadic tribes who roamed Central Asia on horseback. Buddhism may have begun in India, but it too was a passenger on the Silk Road, an idea carried by holy men prepared to travel many thousands of gruelling miles to spread the word.

Around the year AD 540, an Indian Buddhist monk called Bodhidharma – Tamo in Chinese – arrived at a monastery nestled at the feet of Mount Shaoshi. According to the old stories, the monks here spent most of their time translating Buddhist scrolls from Sanskrit into Chinese, and had become so feeble that they'd lost the physical and mental strength needed for hours of meditation. Horrified by their weakness, Tamo taught the monks at Mount Shaoshi how to move as they meditated. Legend has it that these yogalike exercises grew into a form of kung-fu, inspired by the grace and speed of birds and animals. The wonderful, enduring myth of the Shaolin was born: holy men and women who fought to defend the peace of their temple, summoned to the Imperial court by Emperor Gaozong. No one really knows how much of this story is true and how much it has been embroidered over time. Of course, there are some who say the Shaolin really did use their skills to fight and even to kill – and perhaps they are right. Others believe that these gentle, devoted Buddhists simply developed their immense physical skills as an aid to meditation. There is a lot of disagreement over the history of kung-fu, and particularly the Shaolin monks, so I hope the experts will forgive my version of the tale.

By the time Asena and Swiftarrow make their own journey to Chang'an at the height of the T'ang Dynasty, Buddhism had spread throughout China, thoroughly mixing and mingling with traditional beliefs – which is why even as a novice in a monastery, Swiftarrow feels the power of his *chi*, or life-force, and prays to the goddess of the moon, as well as striving to follow the Buddhist Middle Way.

Buddhism was not the only religion to travel the Silk Road – so did Islam and Christianity, and a whole rambling trail of ingenious ideas including the once-hidden Chinese art of making silk, the skills of making paper and glass – and the not-so secret intentions of armies, kings and emperors. But genius and faith were joined on the Silk Road by more deadly passengers – it is thought that the bubonic plague or Black Death reached Europe in this way, carried by fleas trapped in packages of silk and fur.

Over the centuries, hundreds of nomadic tribes have ridden the vast, wild steppes of Central Asia (some still do), and many terrorized the cities, towns and villages of surrounding empires – stealing whatever took their fancy from the grain-stores and treasuries of settled communities. By around AD 550 the Gok Turks ruled an empire from horseback so huge it stretched from the gates of Constantinople in modern Turkey all the way to China. Also known as the Blue Turks, Sky Turks or the Ashina, these fast and deadly riders held firm control over the Silk Road for a number of years. Unfortunately, the Gok Turks left very little of their own written history, so we don't hear much about their side of the story. We do know that the balance of power shifted with the death of their leader, Taspar Khan, fracturing the Gok Turk Empire, and that T'ang dynasty China rose to supremacy, regaining control over the Silk Road.

In the early 1400s, nearly eight hundred years after Swift-arrow and Asena rode away from Chang'an, trade along the Silk Road finally petered out as travel by sea became a more practical option, but centuries later spies were still carrying secrets along paths once trodden by silk-traders. This cat-and-mouse hunt – the Great Game, as it was called – reached its zenith in the 1800s as the British and Russian Empires fought for control of Central Asia. Snaking through great empires and kingdoms that rose and fell over thousands of years, the Silk Road was trodden by many spies and even assassins hired to kill. Most likely, such people are there to this day, scattered across the steppes of Central Asia and the mountainous wilds of Afghanistan, even though the people in charge are not the same.

Finally, the T'ang Dynasty really did see the only female ruler in the entire history of China: the notorious Empress Wu Zetian. Around AD 640, a beautiful thirteen-year-old girl called Wu Zhao arrived at the Imperial palace, personally summoned by Emperor Taizong to join his many concubines. Fifteen years later, the young courtesan had become Empress Wu, ruling at the side of her husband, Emperor Gaozong. Eventually, after he died, the Empress took complete control and even founded her own dynasty, the Zhou. Empress Wu must have been an extraordinary woman to rule a vast empire in an age dominated by men: she took the Imperial throne almost a thousand years before Elizabeth I was crowned Queen of England. To put this in perspective, English women could not even vote in elections until 1928; in China women had no vote till 1949. I wish I could believe that Empress Wu Zetian has been mistreated by history, most of which was written by men who didn't like the idea of a woman in charge. Although it's thought that equality between men and women improved during the reign of Empress Wu Zetian, more than two thousand people met their deaths at her orders, including her own family members – usually as a result of ridiculous charges of corruption and treachery. Personally, I don't buy the old accusation that Empress Wu smothered her own baby daughter in order to frame the Emperor's first wife, Empress Wang, but she certainly held on to power at an extremely high price, and no woman has ruled China since she died in AD 705, more than 1,300 years ago. We will never know what Empress Wu was really like, but I love a good old-fashioned arch-villain and so that is how the Empress appears in *Spirit Hunter*.

Finally, I should say sorry to any readers who know more than I do about Chinese and Central Asian history – you are almost certain to notice the mistakes that I'm likely to have made in my research! I enjoyed this fact-finding mission tremendously but I can't claim to be a scholar.

Acknowledgements

As ever, I'd like to thank my agent and my editors; Catherine Clarke, Denise Johnstone-Burt, Chris Kloet, Ellen Holgate and Clare Baalham. I'm also very grateful to everyone at Walker Books for the huge amount of essential behind-the-scenes work which the outside world never knows about! Thanks also to Sam Llewellyn for helping me over a hurdle, to Jo Macey for her advice on Buddhism, and to Natsegdorje for pointing me in the direction of some excellent books about Central Asian shamanism, or Tengerism. The latter is a fascinating and complicated system of beliefs, which I simplified in places for the sake of my plot, but it's well worth finding out more about it if the interest strikes you.

About the author

Katy Moran is an author with a unique ability for capturing the atmosphere of the times and places she describes, which she attributes to the strong connection she felt to the landscape around her when she was growing up. Katy is now a full-time writer and lives in Shropshire with her husband and son. *Spirit Hunter* is her third novel for children.

Bloodline

In the wild landscape of Dark Age Britain, Essa is abandoned by his father in a lonely marsh-village trapped between two warring kingdoms. Destined to become tangled in the bitter feud, Essa's part in it is more important than he ever dreamed. But how will Essa save those he loves and discover the secret of his true identity when he can trust no one?

Bloodline Rising

Cai, the Ghost, is the fastest, most cunning young criminal in Constantinople. A perfect life, until he is captured, bound and sent to Britain – the home his barbarian parents fled long ago. When he is taken in by Wulfhere, prince of Mercia, Cai soon discovers that his Anglish master knows more about his family than he does. But war threatens and Cai finds he must choose: will he betray his new clan and save himself, or be loyal and risk his life?